# BIG PULP

fantasy | mystery | adventure
horror | science fiction | romance

BILL OLVER Publisher
BILL BOSLEGO Associate Editor

contact: editors@bigpulp.com

**Cover illustration by Ken Knudtsen**

*Visit us online:*
*www.bigpulp.com*
*www.exterpress.com*
*Facebook (Facebook.com/bigpulp)*
*Twitter (twitter.com/BigPulp)*

Submission guidelines are posted online at
http://bigpulp.com/submissions.html

---

**BIG PULP** is available in print online at http://www.exterpress.com/catalog, and in ebook editions through Amazon and Smashwords. Subscriptions available for $40 annually.

**Big Pulp** is distributed by Ingram Periodicals.

**BIG PULP Volume 3, Number 3, September 2012 (Whole issue #6)**

**ISSN # 2167-6046**

**ISBN # 978-0-9836449-4-1**

Published quarterly in March, June, September and December by Exter Press. All credited material is copyright by the author(s). All other material © 2012 Exter Press.

S0-ASC-241

# Table of Contents

## Science Fiction

## Romance

## Fantasy

## Mystery

## Horror

**Cover illustration by Ken Knudtsen**

**Steve Singleman** works in a VA hospital, where he hopes to continue working.

## WE HONOR THOSE WHO SERVE

I've never served, not with my gimpy arm and stiff leg, so I've never been treated by a doctor. I was delivered by a midwife and since then I've been cared for by the pharmacist at Wal-Mart, like everybody else I know. As a civilian employee of the Veterans Administration, I have a pretty good layman's knowledge of medicine, I think, and illegal but affordable access to some drugs and antibiotics. I try to use them to keep myself healthy. Healthy as can be expected nowadays.

I've discovered that if I grind my teeth and press a finger into the fossa just below my ear I can make the chip in my head record whatever I say. Maybe it's because of my cerebral palsy. As far as I know, nobody else here at the VA has been able to do that, though it's not the kind of thing you bring up in chow line. I've decided to use my chip to record an instruction manual for my job.

When I got this job I had to teach myself how to do everything. It's part of the VA way, of course, and has been forever. If you're the only one who knows how to do something important, nobody can fire you, so record nothing. Just common sense. These days, when losing your job most likely means a slow death by starvation or disease, it's more important than ever to cover your ass. But my days are numbered anyway, and I want to do the next guy who gets this detail a favor, so I'm going to use my chip to make a manual of Standard Operating Procedures for a Military Skin Art Archivist, Grade 5, Step 2.

Sergeant Grove is staring at the ceiling over his bed and waiting to die. I figure that thousands of veterans have spent their last hours staring at that same piece of ceiling. No way to know exactly how many, we don't keep a database to record how many vets have died in each bed. While he waits to die, Sergeant Grove mumbles constantly to himself. He can't digest food, move his bowels, urinate, or walk, but he can still talk, if you listen closely. If he wasn't a vet he would have died a couple of decades ago. He's outlived all his family, since they weren't vets, so he doesn't ever have visitors. There are no personal effects in the room, no family photographs, no reading glasses on the end table, no false teeth in a glass, no cane in the corner. Sergeant Grove is the only thing in the room not owned by the Veterans Administration. Sergeant Grove is owned by the Department of Defense.

I review Sergeant Grove's chart at the bedside in preparation for the interview. His real record is in a chip in his head, just like the one in my head, backed up on a database in Colorado Springs, with notes going back to his birth: results of every exam, values of every test of blood and tissue, x-ray images of his plastic knees and MRI images of his ceramic hips. In Colorado Springs there are also frozen sections of his umbilical cord, foreskin, tonsils, wisdom teeth, nasal polyps and colon polyps, preserved samples of the shrapnel in his spine, windshield glass in his face and metal plate in his head, as well as tissue samples of the organs removed and replaced: kidneys, liver, spleen, a foot of colon, a heart valve, and a couple of inches of cerebral artery. The big red folder at his bedside holds only the paper record of this current hospitalization, and a Ziploc bag full of hair. When they shave a vet's head for brain surgery they keep some hair for the mortician, just in case. They'll need it for Sergeant Grove. His anastomosis is leaking and they've decided not to open up his skull again; they're going to let him go. That's when I show up.

◊ ◊ ◊ ◊ ◊

I was a medical records clerk for 30 years in this hospital, but ten years ago I had enough seniority to move into a sweet detail collecting tattoos for the Military Skin Art Archive. The last guy who had this detail kept it until he was 78, but then he couldn't climb the stairs any longer so he had to go. Anybody below GS12 can't take the elevators, and as a civvie he couldn't get his knees replaced. I went to his goodbye party. A lot of people showed up because if you have more than 30 years in they give you a cake. I heard that he hung on almost a year after retirement before he died. That's pretty good, and something to be proud of. Still, I'm a coward, so I don't plan to wait for retirement. I've been saving pills for years. Good ones. They won't be providing cake when I leave this job.

I explain to Sergeant Grove what I'm going to do and offer him the pamphlet that spells out the goals of the Military Skin Art Archive. At one point I think he may actually be hearing me, but it's hard to tell. He slips in and out of orientation, his eyes sometimes focus but more often don't. I confirm his name, rank, DOB and service number, then put the chart back on the end of the bed.

I ask if I can remove his blanket and lift his gown. He mumbles, "Every time I come in for a checkup they take away my pants and put me in a room. It takes weeks to get back out." I take that as a "Yes." He doesn't have much of interest on his front, except the blue banner over his left eyebrow that signifies he was a pre-draft volunteer. That's pretty rare, so I gently pull his scalp back to smooth out his forehead for the jpeg.

I work my way down his body, digitizing the general issue tats, bar code over his sternum, his name over his left nipple, Service number over his right, rank advancement going down the ribs on his left side, tour stripes going down his right side. He's got some smeary Celtic crap on his right arm, or maybe it's barbed wire. That stuff was briefly popular at the beginning of the century. Grade school stuff from before he went into service. I don't bother with it. I roll him over and what I find on his back makes me whistle. Sergeant Grove's memorial tat has four medallions, each for a different theater of operations, which is incredibly rare. The centerpiece of the first medallion, the oldest, is the Iwan of the Badshahi Masjid. Every vet who wears it swears he was there for the siege.

I count the names. Sixty-one names, with fifty-eight more names under the three other medallions. One-hundred and nineteen names. He was a popular guy; you don't get to put a soldier's name on your back unless he's left you permission in his will and testament. Soldiers can only will their names to one memorial, and they tend to give their names to a man they admire and they think will survive to be discharged. Anybody with more than ten names on his back was an exceptional leader, a hero to his men, and anybody with more than twenty names on his back gets archived. Sergeant Grove has one-hundred and nineteen names on his back. Most days I get to nap in my office. Not today.

It will take a while before Sergeant Grove is demobilized. Until he is, I go about my day and wait for the page. I visit with every new inpatient and cruise the clinics. Before they were mandatory, soldiers' tattoos were much more interesting. A young man would spend a year in a foreign land and when it was time to leave he'd get a permanent souvenir to remind himself of the worst time of his life. Years later he'd realize it was the best time of his life, and then that tattoo became his most prized possession. Back then the tats were always something personal, an exotic girl's name, a bottle of the local beer. Now any ink on a man's torso is determined by the Manual of General Operations. I see a lot of the same stuff day after day. Crossed rifles for Infantry, anchors for Navy, bulldogs for Marines, wings for Air Force, trident for Psy-Ops. Text, if it's approved through chain of command, can be worn anywhere on the body, even within inches of rank and tour indicators. Texts that get approved all support the effort: "Death Before Dishonor," "My Business is Death and Business is Good," or my favorite: "Be Vewy Vewy Quiet, I'm Hunting Iwaqis."

As a civilian I'm only allowed one tattoo, the one all VA employees are required to wear, the red box and blue star, with the legend "We Honor Those Who Serve." It's applied after you pass your first year's probation, after they've decided they'll keep you. You can choose where they put it, as long as it is visible outside your clothes. Most employees ask for it to be placed on the backs of their necks, where they can hide it with hair. You don't always want people to know where you work. Sometimes you meet a vet on the street who is pissed off and he'll take out his anger on a civvie VA employee, and God help the civvie who ever swung back at a vet. Sometimes somebody will assume that since you're employed by the Fed you must have something worth stealing. And sometimes it's just not safe to remind people of the government. I chose to have the tattoo placed just under my Adam's apple, where it's always visible. But then, I don't go out much.

Sergeant Snyder's chart says he has "Christmas Dementia." In December and January a lot of vets go crazy just enough to get locked up on the ninth floor. They let the VA keep them warm and fed for a few weeks but as soon as the weather warms up they feel like getting off the lithium and back on the meth, so they miraculously get sane. I don't go up to Mental Health much, because most of the patients up there are not dying, but Sergeant Snyder's intake said he was a full body canvas, and I'm required to photograph those. He is in fact covered completely with ink, but nothing very notable that I can see, just a mash-up of random crap from a dozen different artists. Old faded stuff half covered by bright, new, half finished stuff. His memorial only has three names on it, in a single medallion. I ask him what used to be on his arms, before he got prosthetics.

"Used to have a matched pair of goldfish," he said, "winding up both arms, wrist to elbow. Each fish had exactly one hundred scales, each scale a slightly different color. Got 'em in Okinawa. I loved those goldfish, and so did my wife. She called 'em Yin and Yang, but I called 'em Tit and Taint. Over in the Sandbox I got into the whole left hand below the waist, right hand above the waist thing. Hell, everybody did; you never had any toilet paper. Anyway, my wife sure as hell loved them fish."

"So what happened to the goldfish, Sir?"

"I did three tours in Argentina as a medic. But after three tours I thought I needed to come home and work on my marriage. I told the Army I had nightmares and would kill every gaucho I saw if they sent me back, so they gave me to the National Guard. Didn't work out; we got divorced anyway. I spent ten years working the metal detector outside of West High School, and then some kid's backpack blew up and I lost both arms. That's what happened to my fish."

I wish I'd had a chance to see those fish. There's nothing noteworthy on Sergeant Snyder's body today but he's still awfully proud of his exhibits so I get out the camera, tell him to strip, stand him up against the wall and shoot him.

"Thank you for your service, Sir."

◊ ◊ ◊ ◊ ◊

Private Delaney speaks through a 'voder and sounds like a fly buzzing around inside a tin cup. He leans against the nursing station all day long and nobody can understand a word he says, but you can tell by his eyes that he's telling jokes so all the nurses laugh. There's constant noise coming from the public address speakers, the ones that work anyway. Sometimes words can be distinguished but not often, once in a blue moon a part of a phrase, "…ssssskkkkkshhhcode blue in South ssssshkkkkkkksssssssimmediate assistancessssszkkkkkkssshh…" Most of the noise is just noise. Every piece of equipment on the unit makes some kind of noise, if it's not broken. There is a constant din of beeping pulse oxymeters, high shrill alarms from mobile EKG machines, hissing blood pressure cuffs, ringing phones, and the insistent gongs of the IV pumps. There's a lot of groaning and some shouting, too. Nobody pays any attention to any of the noises. After a few months on the unit you only notice a noise when it stops. At some point Private Delaney stops telling jokes and starts making his slow painful way back to his room. One nurse behind the counter notices the absence of his fly buzz and sticks her head through the narrow window to shout after him, "Thank you for your service, Private!"

I used to do a small trade in side arms. Since handgun possession was made mandatory, you can get a lot for a light, compact pistol in good condition. Every citizen is required to buy at least one handgun from the Military Surplus, but you don't have to carry your government gun all the time. A lot of women don't want to carry around a big ugly .45. The law just says you have to be armed whenever you leave the house. The law does not specify what kind of gun you need to have on you if a cop stops you, so some women will pay a lot for a little .22 or .32, maybe even a single shot novelty gun. Purse guns we used to call them. A lot of the vets are widowers and still have their wives' old guns sitting around the house. I used to trade Percocet for a pistol, and trade the pistol for sex. Of course that was a long time ago, when food was more plentiful, and I was younger. If I got a gun now I would only take food for it.

◊ ◊ ◊ ◊ ◊

War 7 and War 9 seem to be going badly, but there's a downtick of insurgent activity in War 3 that seems like good news. "What's wrong with the color?" asks Private Yoder.

"What do you mean, Sir?"

"The damn color, boy! That man's all orange."

The announcer's hands and face are indeed a funny shade of orange, but his suit and desk and backdrop all look natural. "Maybe that's just his color," I say. "Maybe he's got something."

"Natural, hell! Fix the damn thing."

"How do I do that, Sir?" I want to try to comply, even if it's impossible. I'm a civvie and he's a vet. I owe him a huge debt of gratitude. I have to at least try to do what he tells me to do.

"Find the damn knob! There's a knob, called 'tint' or something."

The screen has no knobs. It's just a screen, it plays all day and all night, and it plays whatever it wants, usually news. Sometimes it'll broadcast an execution, but that's just another kind of news. Still, I reach up behind the screen and pretend to fiddle some knobs. "How's that?"

"Still sucks. Never mind. Not interested in that crap anyway. Stupid, trying to teach civvies what's going on. None of you got a damn brain in your heads."

"Yes Sir. Thank you for your service, Sir."

◊ ◊ ◊ ◊ ◊

It's almost 4 o'clock when I get the page from 5 West. Sergeant Grove is circling the drain.

I've got on an old plastic visor and a rain coat turned around. They're not VA issue; I bought them myself. Mike buttons me up in back. He doesn't wear anything over his clothes. Mike doesn't give a damn about secretions; his clothes are so stiff they crackle when he walks.

Sergeant Grove was demobilized this afternoon. He's just Mr. Grove now. He has not had any medication since he was discharged, so he's pretty alert. That's a shame. I don't have any lidocaine or Percodan to spare. That is usually the case, so Mike and I have a deal. He holds them down for me and I hold them down for him. Folks are pretty amazed at how I can handle the dermatome with only one arm. Nobody taught me, it's the result of years of trial and error, and I botched a lot of tats before I figured out what I was doing. That's the VA way. We get him on his stomach. Mike holds Sergeant Grove's arms over his head, pulling to bring the skin of his back taut. I'm up on the bed, straddling his pelvis.

I like to think my speed with the blade saves them pain, at least duration if not degree. When I'm done he's screamed himself limp. His memorial was huge; I had to flay him from the crack of his butt to the nape of his neck. I've got nothing to put over his wound but the mattress is rubber, and he won't be bleeding for long. We roll him over gently. I'm pretty proud of this part: while they're stunned, exhausted, thinking it's over, I slide in behind their ear and gouge out the records chip with a #3 curette. I'm in and out so fast I've got the chip on the tray with their tat before they react. I cover tat and chip with Gelfoam and draw the sheet of saran over the tray, pop the vacuum tube to shrink wrap it, and put it in the cooler. I lean down and whisper in Mr. Grove's ear: "Thank you for your service, Sir." Then I'm ready to hold him down for Mike.

Mike starts on the left knee and before he's got the patella off Mr. Grove is dead. Shock and blood loss, a relatively peaceful death for a man who's survived what Mr. Grove survived. I let go of Mr. Grove's wrists and help Mike manipulate the leg to expose the cruciate ligaments. It's not part of my job, but I'm finished for the day and Mike is a good friend. I can't take off my raincoat until Mike helps me, anyway.

Holding Mr. Grove's skinny leg in flexion I watch Mike do his work. He's a butcher compared to me, but then again he's got a lot more stuff to cut off than I do. And he's got somewhere he goes in the evenings, somewhere and something he's never told me about, so late afternoons like this one he's always in a hurry. He's got the wire cutters in one hand and the bone saw in the other and he's got two plastic buckets at his feet that rapidly fill up with salvaged parts. I'm glad I'm wearing the visor and raincoat; it's wet in there. Housekeeping will need to use the hose.

I like to leave a tidy office behind me at the end of my watch. Squared away, the vets call it. You never know if you're going to be the next person who opens your top right hand desk drawer, or if it will be somebody from GSA or the next guy who gets your detail. I think a lot about preparations these days. I'm coughing a lot, and the stairs are harder to climb every day. I get lightheaded sometimes, and I know I need to have my wits about me to end my career in the VA the way I want to. I need to have my wits about me, and some strength left in my one good arm.

The memorials have to be harvested right down to the hypodermis, and while the flesh is still living, to ensure viable DNA.

The Archive only wants the biggest memorials, because a man with a hundred names on his back, a man like the late Sergeant Grove, is a true warrior. You get a memorial like that by surviving battles on four continents, by fighting with everything from nukes to sticks. You survive starvation and long marches and every kind of disease there is. You follow orders, and the men around you are willing to follow the orders you give. Men like that are just what this country will need when it gets back on its feet. We'll need an army of men like Sergeant Grove. That's what the Military Skin Art Archive was designed to do. Preserve the best of the best.

I've worked for the Archive for a very long time. I know how it works. The process is mostly automated at the Archive end. Tats come in from all over the VA system and they're put in cold storage as soon as they arrive. Nobody ever really looks at them.

When the time comes, I'll spread the lidocaine on my neck and take a handful of Percodans. I'll use the dermatome to harvest my tat, the blue box, We Honor Those Who Serve. It's right under my Adam's apple, where I can see it in the mirror. All the way down to the hypodermis, to preserve viable DNA. Gelfoam to stop the bleeding. I'll dig my chip out from under my ear and leave it in the top right hand desk drawer for you to find. The trick will be to stay conscious long enough to get the job done.

I'll freeze my tat and ship it to Colorado Springs and they'll archive it like any other. A little piece of me will be in the permanent collection, alongside the best men we've ever produced. Some day somebody who looks just like me will have a role to play in rebuilding this nation. And somebody will thank him for his service.

**Conda V. Douglas** has recently been published in *Fangtales* and in two anthologies, *Untied Shoelaces of the Mind* and *An Eclectic Collage, Volume II.* Conda most recently appeared in **Big Pulp** in the Fall 2011 issue, with "Blood Tells," a tale of Irish horror.

## THE PAWN'S DANCERS

Jameson came at me, his knife raised. Rage masked his face, making him a stranger. I screamed and awoke with echoes tearing my throat. I reached out to touch Jameson lying next to me.

He wasn't there.

Grey light filtered through the window, crazed with a jagged film. Touching it, my fingertips destroyed the film pattern. I gasped at the cold wet surprise.

A shadow obscured the light. Jameson. I half expected to see the knife in his hand. A special knife used to filet a special type of animal that only swam in water and never came on land, I remembered now.

"You awake?" Jameson asked.

I sat up and shook my head to clear it. Was it the past I remembered or the future? I slept so much these days.

Jameson stared out the window. He never spoke of his past. He couldn't. I didn't know how he came to lead the expedition. For all our physical heat, he remained as cold to me as the odd coating that glazed the window.

His white hair shone, reflecting the overhead light. I closed my eyes and saw mounds of white lying upon the ground.

"What is the white cold that falls from the sky?" I asked.

Jameson frowned.

"I saw it, in my dreams."

"Impossible," Jameson said. "Who contaminated you?"

"How would I know if someone contaminated me?" I said.

"Somebody did, No Name."

Jameson sat down beside me. He touched my face and the bitter cold between us cracked. "I'm trying to protect you," he said.

"From contamination? Or from something else? Why is my remembering so strange now?"

He stood, breaking the connection between us.

"You know the law," he said, his voice rough, jagged. It made me think of the frozen water upon the window and how the cold had cut into my finger.

"Don't ask questions," I said. "Don't try to learn to read or write. And don't talk to anybody who's born not made, not even my lover." I couldn't keep the anger out of my voice. Yet I still didn't know why I was angry.

Jameson winced at my jabbing words.

"There's so many laws I can't remember them all," I said.

"Wait here," he said.

"I know how to wait," I said. "I wait for you to return to camp. I wait to remember. I wait to live. Nothing has been brought to me for days. What am I waiting for?"

"You'll only make it worse."

"I'm afraid." I wrapped my arms around myself and hugged, drawing little comfort and less heat.

Jameson sighed. He sat down next to me and added his warmth. "You're what we call 'bleeding.' When a memorist recalls too much, not only objects, but when the past bleeds into the present. Do you understand?"

He continued without waiting for me to answer. "The natural barriers break down in your mind." He stared at the knife in his hands. "The past bleeds through, destroying your sense of reality. The final disease of memorists."

He stood.

"Wait," I said. I grabbed his arm, stiff and cold beneath my fingers. "What will happen now? What will I remember?"

Jameson shook his head. He pulled away. Then he left, gone to the excavation site, leaving me behind. As always.

I paced. On a table lay a stone. Picking it up, I remembered my arrival.

◊ ◊ ◊ ◊ ◊

My heart had thumped in an echo to my steps as I walked off the ship. I'd first seen Jameson standing, a warm wind lifting his white hair. I didn't know his name then. His name came after his knowledge of my body.

He had stared at me, unblinking. Did my face betray me as a freak?

He led me to a place where unidentified objects lay scattered on tables. I had stumbled into a chair and sat, dazed, surrounded by light and smell and color and texture, so different from my life of grey walls before.

Dirt still clung to the ancient artifacts of long dead lives. I didn't want to touch any of them, didn't want to remember their locked away pasts, their dead memories. I started to cry.

Jameson placed his hand on my shoulder.

"Here," he said, giving me the stone, "it'll help."

I had stared at the stone, uncomprehending.

"It's as if you can see the soul of the past, like you can see the color in the opal." It was the only time he was to name anything.

I remembered. I remembered the glorious stones with the captured light dancing in a sunbeam. The vision gave me the courage to pick up a piece of twisted metal.

I stared at it for long moments. My heart beat even faster, harder. Would I be able to do what I was created for?

My eyes tight shut, I took a breath. There. A knowing of what the metal scrap was settled into my mind.

"This was part of a water remover on the front window of people transport machinery."

Jameson had patted my hand. "Good. You figured it out." He

smiled.

I'd smiled, too.

◊ ◊ ◊ ◊ ◊

Now I set the opal down, not wanting to remember any more. The cold chewed close to my heart. The silence vibrated with my fear.

My fear too strong to ignore, I pulled on a coat and followed Jameson.

I headed toward the excavation site.

Our camp squatted on one side of a large lake, the excavation site on another side. Something grey and thick rose in tendrils from the lake. I reached out to grasp a tendril and met only air. Wet, cold air.

Through the grey, I spotted a distant figure standing across the lake, sheltered in the trees. It seemed too large, too bulky, to be any member of the expedition.

The person raised an arm and beckoned.

"Hey, No Name," Mayer called from behind me.

I turned toward her and when I looked back the figure had disappeared.

Mayer ran toward me, stumbling over the rocky lake shore. Her hair bristled in tufts over her scalp as if she were some alarmed wild animal. Or someone who saw a ghost. Me.

She clambered next to me and grasped my arm for support.

I smoothed down one of her errant cowlicks. Most expedition members avoided contaminating me by avoiding me altogether. Except Mayer. She gave me my name that is not a name. No Name, the only name I possess.

Any knowledge distorts my remembering, muddying the empty waters of my mind. Even proper names conjure up images. Without a name I grew up with others of my kind and all we learned was to remember.

"Where's everyone?"

"At the site, of course. Where you should not be," she said. "Or here."

"Look." I took out my lucky piece. I kept little items, like this and the tiny box of fire sticks, in my pocket.

"You should have turned that in," Mayer said.

"It's a pawn."

"What?"

"That's what it's called."

"Memorists don't recall names. Who contaminated you?" Not me, her eyes said, not this time.

"No one."

"Do you know what it's for?" Mayer asked, her interest caught. She brushed her hands through grey and brown streaked hair.

I rolled the small wood piece in my hand. The first item ever brought to me which I couldn't identify. I'd worked with it for hours, until Jameson said, "You can't remember them all."

Painted black, it fascinated me with its unusual shape, a flattened base and a round ball on top. It takes something I can see and touch for me to remember. If the piece has no practical function, then I can't recognize it.

"I almost have it," I said, "when I hold the pawn I see squares, odd, but—"

"Stop it," Mayer said. "Please don't do this."

"Why? It's my job, like you with your reptiles."

"It's not your job, it's what you are," Mayer said. She looked angry. She sounded afraid. "You weren't born, you were made. Remember that." I didn't know if she was talking to me or herself.

"I won't forget. How could I?"

"There are no reptiles to study here," Mayer said, not answering. She looked out over the lake as if she could see the city that once crouched on the lake's shores. "It's the cold."

The cold crept round my ankles, cutting to the bone. The last of the sunlight flashed over the lake waters, golden rays with no warmth. Ice lurked on the rocks and made walking treacherous. The cold seemed a waking beast, stretching out claws to snag and tear.

"The coming of the cold, that's why, don't you see?" Mayer said.

"The coming of the cold?" I asked. "Isn't it only another season?"

"It's not only winter," Mayer said and then realized she'd contaminated me. She ran her hands through her hair. "No, you don't understand, you're only a memorist." She twisted away from me, her arms crossed, a dark mottling at the base of her neck.

*Winter.* I rolled the new word in my mind. Savoring it.

I glimpsed the lake covered in a deep sheet of always frozen water. A memory? Or what was to come?

"My remembering, I've always been able to control it. Now it controls me. Help me, Mayer." I clutched the little wooden piece tight, drawing strength from it.

Mayer said, sharp, but with no force behind her words, "Go back to the camp and wait for us." She ran, not looking at me, dismissing me.

"Mayer?" I called.

Hurrying after her, I stumbled and fell. The ice ripped into my hands as I caught myself.

In my reflection in the ice, I saw Mayer's face imposed over mine, her hair solid brown, and I knew that once she had looked so. I remembered, her grey hair meant she was older. Was the world growing old? Was that what was so wrong? Or was it only the expedition that had grown old?

Blood from my cut hands had smeared around the ice, around my face. I remembered Jameson and the dream.

Then, in the ice, I saw reflected buildings glittering with lights, a city long since vanished. I listened close and city sounds came to me, a distant, ancient rumble. I reached out and touched the reflection. The city shattered, ice crackling under my fingertips.

I shivered, not from the cold, and stumbled on. Ahead I saw the bright glare of the excavation lamps used for evening work. Their glowing cast a welcoming light, so different from the dead city lights I had remembered.

I reached the tents set up over the dig and hesitated. I had never visited the site before, being relegated always to waiting at the permanent camp.

The main tent enclosed the remaining wall of an excavated building. Shadowed figures moved in and out of the circle of lamp light. Faces flared into focus, distorted by the glare. The light threw confusing shadows upon the ancient wall, as if reflecting a struggle of trapped animals.

Activity clustered around a long table. Half packed boxes stood on the table, along with artifacts. When people saw me, they moved away from the table and into the shadows. I knew their faces but not their names, for they always acted thus, as if the curse of being a memorist might be catching.

Mayer bent over some objects on a table, intent on her work, wrapping something in packing material. The light elongated her face.

Every moment with her was only an isolated incident with someone who remained a cipher, a sketch with no coloring or detail. I wondered if I was as elusive to her as she was to me.

I touched her shoulder.

She slumped lower with my touch, as if she could not bear the weight of my hand.

"We have so little time left," she said, not looking up.

"It's me. No Name."

Mayer jerked her head up and stared at me. "Leave while there is still time."

Jameson came up behind me and grabbed my arm.

"No," Mayer said.

"You're not allowed on site," Jameson said. His harsh growl made me flinch.

"I followed Mayer. I have to know how to stop the bleeding."

Jameson sighed. He sat down next to Mayer, not trusting his knees, an old man. He picked up a knife and turned it over in his hands. "It happens to all memorists, sooner or later. After the last one, the one before No Name, I told them not to send any more memorists. They ignored me and sent her."

"You didn't have to take No Name into your bed," Mayer said, as if I wasn't there, no longer existed.

"I didn't know how young and beautiful she would be." Jameson said.

"Too young for you," Mayer said.

"I hoped this time would be different," Jameson said. "Now she'll destroy everything. She's like the others."

He sounded so bereft I wanted to sit next to him and stroke his hair as I used to do. But I feared the knife in his hands and how they spoke as if I were already dead.

"I'm afraid," I said. *And I'm still here, alive,* I wanted to add.

"They always are," Jameson said. "What difference does it make now?" He kept turning the knife in his hands.

I wanted to run from that sharp blade. I looked at the old wall. Flecks of faded paint still clung to the wall, shadows. Or memories.

Jameson kept talking. His words faded from my hearing. The wall, as I watched, changed.

The wall stood complete, a brilliant mural's glowing color splashed across it. The mural represented a large vehicle with lettering along its side. People appeared, sitting in chairs against the wall, their faces impassive in a place where no one stays or belongs.

"No Name?" Jameson's voice floated out of nowhere.

I heard the rumble of the buses arriving, the heavy oily stink of ozone in the air, and the murmur of voices long silent. The dead faces crowded around me, speaking long dead words.

One ghost reached out to me. It was Jameson, knife raised in his hand.

I screamed and ran. I ran with the heavy black of asphalt beneath me, the blaring of horns and screeching of tires, and the glare of city lights blinding me. I ran through the streets of a city long since vanished.

Icy fingers reached out and tore at my face. Sobbing, I fell.

Light scratches of icy cold on my face, like tiny caresses, roused me. I looked up and saw the branch that had whipped my face as I ran past.

Touching the melting drops on my face I thought of frozen tears. More frozen tears fell all around me, tiny sparkles of white slanting through the trees.

Snow, I remembered, my first snow. Another image came to me, of a too still figure cloaked beneath a cold white blanket.

My legs trembled as I stood. I searched for the lights of the camp or site. I recognized no sign to lead me home.

"Mayer," I called. I waited. No answering shout. Silence greeted me. Silence growing heavy with the snow fall. I yelled till my voice failed and listened again. Nothing.

Whimpering, I tried not to cry. Then I remembered.

In my mind, flames flared, warm, inviting, a sanctuary from the killing snow. I smelled the sweet tang of burning resin, heard the tiny explosions of pitch, and reached out to the promised safety of the fire. I touched only the wet falling snow.

Hurry, a voice whispered in my mind. Panic sent me searching the ground for tree branches.

Then, in a small clearing, there stood a huge pine tree. No branches on this goliath grew near the ground and its huge trunk created a natural windbreak. Sanctuary.

I cleared the dry ground beneath the tree of pine needles and cones, piling them and my branches. Remembering.

I pulled the box of miniature fire sticks from my pocket, praying that the centuries had not destroyed their special ability.

I took one of the little sticks—matches—I remembered now, and struck it on the rough side of the box. A pinpoint of fire appeared on the end of the stick and this I touched to the gathered wood. The wood flared alight, memory becoming reality.

For the first time in my life I created something. Fire.

I leaned against the massive tree trunk, seeking comfort in the rough bark. For inside me grew a cold feeling that no fire could dispel. How could I remember so much? The city, then the name of the tree, how to build a fire, why could I remember all this and more?

The cold questions came. Did Jameson attack me, or was that another distortion of my remembering? Why did no one follow me, try to help me? Did I matter so little?

To dispel my chilling thoughts, I huddled close to the fire's lifesaving warmth, adding wood to keep it burning strong.

I stared into the flames, fascinated with the fire's leap and flutter, like a live thing. Sparks flew upward through the pine tree branches. My remembering seemed as those sparks, flashes of random light. I wondered if the flames of my ability would burn away my mind.

As the night progressed the snow stopped and the stars spun across the sky, serene. I moved around to stay awake, ate some snow, tended the fire and waited for morning. I brought out my pawn and held it for comfort.

Until I remembered and rage burned through my chest, the anger warming me as a fire could never do. Then I forced the pawn deep into a pocket, wanting to forget.

Near morning I dozed, exhausted. I dreamt of dancers beyond the dying glare of my fire. I heard the stamping of feet, the rustling of the brush as they danced. A low muted hum, a chant, hovered in the air.

In the flickering light, I recognized faces from my childhood. Faces now older, grown to adulthood. Faces that smiled beneath furred hoods.

One dancer came into the circle of my firelight. Dressed in rough clothing unlike anything I had ever seen before, black hair long and braided, she stepped close. The fire outlined her features and I saw my own face, smiling back at me. I reached out toward the dancer, wanting to touch the joy in her face, and awoke to dawn.

The morning sun light streaked through the tree branches, illuminating where I was, warming me. Already the snow melted, a false winter start. I started walking.

I broke out of the trees and saw the camp within easy walking distance close by. Had they not seen my fire burning? Why did no one come?

I started toward camp and there, on the path in front of me, a snake. I stifled a scream as I saw it coil, preparing to strike, deadly, not two feet from me.

"There are no rattlers here," I whispered, "Mayer told me." With my words I could see through the snake, to the ground beneath. The snake faded, replaced by a branch. I called the snake back, then reached out and touched its reptile skin and felt rough bark.

"Ghosts, only ghosts," I said. I'd learned how to tell the difference between remembered and real.

When I reached camp, it appeared deserted. Weary, I trudged to my room.

As I stared down at my meager possessions piled on the bed I remembered how the dancers came out of the night with the promise of a beginning.

I packed with a confidence I'd never known, picking out the necessary items, discarding the rest, the leavings of my old life. I remembered everything I might need, remembering last a compass. I did not intend to lose my way again.

Jameson surprised me as I stood over the bed, packing my few personal items into a box.

"What are you doing?" he asked. He stared at me, his mouth working, an old man with no teeth. No bite. Or so I believed until I saw the knife in his hand.

"Leaving," I said. Anger kept my fear tethered.

"You can't," he said. His words rang with rage, though whether at me or himself, I wasn't sure.

"I'm learning to control it, the bleeding," I said.

He raised the knife. "That's what they all said."

I grasped his wrist, twisting. His skin felt cold, as if he lived the winter of his life. The bones shifted beneath my fingers. With a cry he dropped the knife.

Beneath his age, I saw a young man appear, a man with a mop of curly red hair and an easy smile. Jameson's younger self so little resembled him that I couldn't believe it was the same person. Perhaps it was not.

He frowned and his younger self faded away, leaving only the old shell. "I couldn't let you run away to die alone. I love you." He looked at the knife in my hand.

"It's not love," I said. I wanted to shake him. "Don't you see? Bleeding isn't a destruction of my ability. It's a natural development. You said yourself that it happens to all the memorists."

A thundering crash came from outside, nearby.

"They're tearing down the permanent structures," I said, with sudden understanding.

"We're closing up the site, it's played out." Jameson said. "All of us, except you, have grown old and out of date. Relics. And you—"

"—are bleeding. Useless."

Jameson put his head in his hands.

I left him, an old defeated man, there.

I left the permanent camp, slipping away under the cover of the camp's destruction.

Mayer found me at the edge of the lake.

"No Name," she called. Not my name, not anymore.

I waited for her. I owed her a farewell.

"Where are you going? You can't survive alone."

"I can't survive with Jameson," I said, remembering an old lost man who did not understand.

Mayer flinched. "I'll keep you safe from him," she said.

"You no longer need to save me," I said. "Besides, there is nothing for me here."

"Don't worry," she said, coming to me and putting her arms around me as she had so often in the past, "I'll take care of you, No Name.

You'll be retrained."

"Is that what happened to the other memorists?" I asked, thinking of the dancers I had seen. Of the missing faces from the dance.

"I don't know," Mayer said, her chin tucked low.

She lied. She did know. I pulled away from her grasp.

I reached into my pocket and drew out the little wooden piece.

"This pawn is a piece from a game called chess. Pawns are early sacrificed during the game. Easily lost and forgotten." I flung the pawn far out over the water and did not look to see where it fell.

Mayer stared at me. "Some memorists ran away, escaped," she said. "I thought they had not survived. Now I am not so sure."

"It doesn't matter. I'll remember how to live," I said.

Mayer hugged me. "I will not tell them which way you went."

I headed south along the lake. When I reached the southern edge, I paused and looked over the lake, glimpsing the city that once was there. I rinsed my face in the icy water to break the spell.

When the ripples ceased I stared at my reflection.

The lake water was clear to the bottom. My remembering had always been like looking into a well of dark roiling water. Now the water calmed.

There was one other thing I might have told Mayer. Though I believe she already knows. One thing I remembered.

I remembered I was home.

**WC Roberts** lives in a mobile home up on Bixby Hill, on land that was once the county dump. The only window looks out on a ragged scarecrow standing in a field of straw and dressed in WC's own discarded clothes. WC dreams of the desert, of finally getting his first television set, and of ravens. Above all, he writes, and has had poems published in *Strange Horizons*, *Apex*, *Space & Time Magazine*, *Mindflights*, *Aoife's Kiss*, **Big Pulp**, *Star\*Line*, and others.

---

## FAMILY ALBUM

data streaming
from the eye of Hubble
our grandfather shows what has
or might have been

we look back
tics and cultured senility
a string of pearls gone down the well
for a sip

a convalescent star
limping onward and down
the wormhole studded with malformed planets
and a gaseous giant

gazing into the abyss
his navel, the center of the universe, himself
anxious, in our last days, to reassemble
avengers of thirst

**Sharon Kae Reamer** has been published most recently in *Port Iris Magazine* and the *Transtories Anthology* from Aeon Press. Her novel *Primary Fault*—a tale of seismology, druids, and an evil blonde—was published in July 2012 by Terrae Motus Books.

---

## FOR NOW, HOWEVER, THE DRAGONS HAVE FREE REIN

The sun blazed with midsummer hot but couldn't compare with the lights. They flashed through the living room windows, and then she was gone.

When my mother came back in, she was different.

Chandler hugged her knees. "Mommy, you saw the lights! Just like on teevee. Are you going on teevee? Did they say 'the universe is trying to kill you'?"

The reality show always started with the announcer saying those words. I knew when I heard those words it was time for sit-still-and-listen behavior.

Mom looked at me. "Did you let Chandler watch that show again?" Her lips had stretched out like she was about to give me a spanking.

My brother couldn't say 'universe'. It came out 'oonibus' instead. Mom didn't spank me. She reached out to smooth my brother's sun-bleached hair but then stopped and clenched her hands.

"Yes, Chandi, I'm going somewhere like that. But you," she glanced at me, "and Sandia can't tell anyone. The truth is dangerous."

Chandi and I ran outside, dashing here and there, but the lights had vanished. I sat on the swing. He dug in the sand. The Standard Model of our universe contained just two particles—me and him. He ate dirt. I tried to clip him with the swing. He didn't notice until nearly too late and shoved me sideways. I yelled, "The universe is trying to kill you," and wrestled him into the sand.

Father's catamaran appeared on the horizon. He rode up with the roaring tide, the retreating sun making his sail glow. We ran out to help him beach it, jostling each other for a hug and some kind words.

"How was your day, little ones?" He hugged us with strong Daddy arms.

Chandler spat out his words. "Mom met the lights. But we couldn't find them. They just went away."

Dad looked at me. I nodded. "She acted funny afterwards."

"Sandia said that they were hiding. But if they're hiding, we should be able to find them, right, Dad?"

I peeked up at Dad, making my eyes into slits to look more grown up. "What is it? The lights. Is it a car?"

Dad pulled us in close as we marched up the ridge. "No, not a car, but no one can see it who's not supposed to. It's a container bigger than a catamaran and smaller than a mouse all at the same time."

Chandler screamed with laughter. "A mouse as big as a catman. I'd like to see it move!"

Dad smiled at Chandler's not being able to say catamaran, but his eyes looked sad.

I wanted to ask more, but we'd reached the front door. Dad's arms dropped from our tanned shoulders to hang limp at his side while he scuffed the sand from his sandals.

Mom sat in the living room with all the shades pulled, her hands folded in her lap. She didn't look up, not even at Dad.

"What's for dinner, what's for dinner," Chandler sang, dancing around the room.

He didn't get it, that something was wrong with Mom.

"Settle down, Chandi, I need to talk to your mother."

Dad stood there, all tightened up, like he was about to dive into cold, rough surf. Chandler's singing had that annoying sharp edge to it. Dad sat beside Mom on the couch.

I stood in front of Chandler, arms crossed to block his way. He screamed at me.

"Didn't I tell you kids to settle down?"

That calmed my brother. I dropped to the floor and dragged him with me so they would forget we were there. My father talked in quiet tones, telling my mother about the usual quantum physics stuff at the lab. Today they made the brane vibrate enough to generate the waves that could be powered up to use as a multi-dimensional trap against the dragons.

Finally he asked her, "Do you want to talk about it?"

Dad held her hand, tight, like Mom did with us whenever we crossed a busy street. She smiled at him. Her face had that happy look she wore when they thought we weren't watching.

Chandler puffed at a displaced sand cricket. "The oonibus is trying to kill you," he hissed as the bug tried to escape.

The TV show told stories about people who had seen the lights. They disappeared after. Sometimes they came back, but then they weren't alive anymore, or they wore their insides on the outsides. I put my hands over Chandler's eyes when they showed that, even though they didn't show it up close.

"I met a man, at least he still looked like one," Mom said. "He said I've got the kernel inside me."

Dad looked down.

"I have to go."

"Who was it?"

She shook her head. "I don't know. Doesn't matter now, does it?"

"When do you have to leave?"

"Right away."

"How—"

She put a finger to his mouth. "I asked him. He said it's not true. The show. It's all different...there."

"Don't—"

"Keep working on that trap." Mom took her hand from Dad's, sliding her fingers slowly across his palm.

The show's announcer always explained at the end. About how after the accident, after the fabric of space split—but Dad said that wasn't right, you can't split something that's not even there, but they still didn't know what happened—they relocated the lab south of the border. That's where my dad and the others work to try and contain the dragons—those scientists who had gotten caught—who were part of the nonexistent fabric of space and who weren't quite human any more.

The narrator's last line always made me shiver, almost as much as the first one, the line Mom spoke as she walked away. A thin ridge of red welts trailed down her neck and back. They looked like dragon scales. They pulsed. I put my hands over Chandi's eyes.

He chanted it, at the same time Mom did. "For now, however, the dragons have free rein."

Stephen D. Rogers is the author of *A Dictionary of Made-Up Languages*; a member of the Language Creation Society and the New England Science Fiction Association; and the award-winning author of more than 700 shorter pieces.

---

# JOB POSTING

"Must speak a language"
Legally excluded
Telepaths
Who gathered in tatters
Rousing the rabble
Silently

**J.M. Sirrico** is pursuing the writing life, creating fiction and non-fiction for children and adults. She holds a Masters' Degree in Library Science, but works part-time jobs outside of this field to support her writing habit. Cape Cod, MA is the beautiful place she calls home.

## WIDOW IN RED

Grandma wore red to my graduation party.
Staggering into the room she paralyzes my friends, rupturing our
    laughter.
She stalks me until we stand nose to nose, at the center of everything.

"If she's here, I'm leaving!"
Aunt Helen showed up and Grandma saw red;
redder than the red of the polyester dress that reveals all her curves
    from neck to knee.
She pummels the words, tipping her glass of Jameson's for emphasis.

I reach for the glass. "Gram," I redirect, "have you met my friends?"
She drags her cigarette, examines the white filter tattooed by her
    painted lips,
then drops it into the drained glass; sizzling impotently.

Leading, I cradle her elbow.
We sweep the room, scenting a trail of Channel No 5.
"Yeah, yeah," small puffs of smoke punctuate her disinterest,
"I've met them all," waving a wrist.
"Except…"

Her eyes land on a chest clothed in blue plaid.
"Who is this handsome young man?"
Exhaling gray smoke, she bats her eyelashes and primps her newly
    dyed jet-black hair.

Moving towards him Grandma holds her hands out to Mark, Sally's
     boyfriend.
Pulling at his waistband Mark stands and extends a hand in greeting;
his dark Irish looks redolent of my long deceased grandfather.
"Hello Mrs. O'Brien," Mark greets.
"Mrs. Robinson's more like it," Sally mutters.
Grandma takes Mark's hand between both of hers
and starts rubbing.

After the party, in completely unrelated events,
Sally dumps Mark.
Grandma hires him to landscape the yard behind her cottage.

The evening after he finishes Grandma reaches into the top drawer of
     her dresser.
A scarlet silk negligee flows across the lip of the drawer revealing
     light wood underneath.
Three crisp, hundred dollar bills, tucked beneath the negligee for
     emergencies,
are gone.

# THE FIX

We sit.
"I'm going to sit next to you for just thirty seconds," I say.
"You are sitting next to me."
I slide over so our bodies touch. "I mean, really next to each other."
"Why?"
"So I can get my fix of you, just 30 seconds."

Rhythmic, time moves quickly and far beyond my 30 seconds.
People appear on the path.
They will see us touching.
They may know my father or mother or brother
or
they walk by.

We stand.
You step closer.
Your hands take hold of my hips
caress without moving
claiming their place.

Strong arms pull me towards you.
I am lost, held in your eyes.
Your left hand moves to my neck,
gently, firmly your thumb holds my chin in place.
Breath suspended, eyes closed, lips poised,
your fingers squeeze slightly.
I feel the warm, hard
resistance
of your wedding ring.

Cecelia Chapman investigates the human hunger for adventure, mystery, and illusion using video, still image, and short and graphic fiction in works that examine the way we think and live.

## NOT FOR LONG

When Hugo recognized me, he was drunk. That was after his woman companion left him at the bar. He said he was staying in a hotel down the beach and sat drinking and talking to me until my shift was over. A busboy helped me walk him up the hill where he passed out in my hammock. But he was not the addict and alcoholic rumors made him. My previous soft-fleshed, bratty-boy employer was a hard-boned man. Thick, scarred hands made sandpaper sounds as he clenched them while he slept.

One key in his pocket. Wallet with one black credit card. Cuban passport, completely blank, except for one rubber-stamp seal of a jaguar in a bleeding tree, a smiling baby in its mouth, marking his entry into the country yesterday and a date of birth making midnight, two hours ago, the first minute of his thirty-seventh year alive. Pale blue handkerchief with the initial A. Bespoke olive linen jacket with a welt under the left arm. Denim pants. Woven leather sandals from Guatemala on thick calloused feet that did not need shoes. Tissue-thin pink Uluwatu t-shirt.

I was picking through him when he opened one eye, laughed at me and passed out again. I felt he understood I was doing this because I brought him into my home. And for my other more personal reasons. Second-hand stories followed him; obsession, loss of a software fortune, his rough, handsome wife named Allison, a complicated divorce trial, his disappearance, then rare sightings that were like jokes.

Watching him through the night, from my bed in the corner of a large and quiet rented studio apartment that I liked and where I worked as an artist, out to his hammock on the terrace, all I thought was I didn't want to regret bringing him home.

Foreign yachts with sails like torn wings jockeyed into harbor early. Winds sliced open a black crack on the horizon, a sliver of darkness in the red dawn widened, as if night had won.

*"I saw her again."* We'd walked down the beach, gone in the sea, returned to the apartment to breakfast and talked more.

*"Who?"* I hung my laundered work shirt on a clothesline where it sailed in the breezes, dry by the time I poured coffee and offered Hugo slabs of papaya with lime.

*"The woman I saw that everyone said I didn't see. I'm going to tell you something. Then, forget it. I went for a run. It was a beautiful day. I had only one care that morning and that was that I was afraid I was losing Allison. I took time off work, we planned the rest of the day together. We made love earlier."* He paced the terrace balcony, leaning over the rail, watching the street. *"I asked her if she wanted to go running with me. She said she'd wait in bed."*

Cards printed with bleeding hearts and pierced with arrows were tied in trees and posts that lined the threatened parade route. They made a whirring, rattling sound in the winds. Some came loose, flopping on the terrace like fish thrown on wet sand, slap of flesh. Scarlet flamboyant flowers were ripped off in the winds, they covered everything, like a petal carpet of spilled blood on my floor every morning.

*"On the run, in the hills, I found a woman fallen on the ground. She was warm, breathing, but unconscious. I covered her with my sweatshirt. Running back I found people with a cell phone, they called an ambulance. When I returned to the woman, she was gone."*

*"That should have been alright. But a beautiful woman is hard to forget. I told Allison. Not that I thought the woman was beautiful, but that I had found her, then, that she was gone, and that is why it took me so long to return. She laughed at me. Allison laughed. I felt*

34

disturbed, disoriented. I still remember the way she turned over, got out of bed, laughing."

Long before, this religious festival was a rain celebration involving human sacrifice in jungle ruins surrounded for miles with carved rock rattlesnakes the size of a curled-up man. One day all the snakes disappeared. Later I saw them in the museum in the capitol, dozens of them. In that cold white room they seemed immediately real, more alive than in the bush, fleshless, angry creatures. When I returned later to show them to a friend I could not find them anywhere.

"The day was ruined, Allison distant. I can't remember what I did. Shortly after that I started drinking, later heavily...other things...I made bad hiring choices, an employee who embezzled, another sold information. Then Allison left. She divorced me, she took the company. She proved I was incompetent. Well, no, first I just didn't show up for three weeks. When I finally made it to work, a guard stopped me from entering. When Allison sold the company I was in jail for fraud. My father died suddenly, the shock, I never saw him..."

"...none of that matters now. I went south and drank hard for a year. Hit bottom, got sick. Finally all I could do was gut fish for a living, later I fished...I was in a bar when a ship comes in, a sailing vessel...sleek, maybe 50 crew, big money just floating in. Fishermen are laughing and yelling at the women walking down the ramp. This is the first time they have seen this, women who want women, in a group like this, entering their port, their town. The women are holding hands, arms around each other, in shorts, barely shirts. Fishermen are yelling 'make me captain!' The owner of the boat I'm working on points and says he wants that pair. It's Allison. With that woman I saw on the ground. They got into a taxi."

"I borrowed a friend's taxi fast. They weren't hard to find. I spent a couple of hours watching the hotel beach deck where my ex-wife and the woman were drinking, bickering, kissing, rubbing sun tan lotion on each other, holding hands. It lasted an eternity of hell. I thought my anger would burn me in the taxi, the whole taxi, just ignite it, or *attract lightning. Gone in flames, like that. I thought a lot of things, I remembered a lot more. I would have gone in, maybe bought them a drink, but I smelled and I'm not happy in bars with white canvas tents and umbrellas any more, and the way I was feeling, well, I'd just better stay low. Eventually they went looking for a taxi."*

*"I took them back to their ship. Allison got out of the taxi first. Not a glance at me. The other women paid, looking me over, hungry. So I pushed up my dark glasses. She backed out fast. I lived off her look for a long time."*

Hugo parsed sea, jungle and street. Big girls slinking through town in holiday dresses, sexy with special red lips, holding hands with little girls carrying the lunch chicken home by its wrung neck. Tourists at cafe tables drinking breakfast beers, waiting to record the procession with small devices in their hands. Little boys racing all over. Men talking outside the bar. Nuns crossing the graveyard, the church square. Women stopped in the bakery door, blocked by a boy pulling a horse spooked by the cards snapping and whistling in high winds. The balloon man twisted a jaguar from a balloon, enigmatic screeches erupting from the felt tip marker passage across taut latex leaving hieroglyphic spots, teeth, bloody claws.

*"I was broke, living day-to-day. But I had rent money from fishing on charters, local commercial boats hired me. Sometimes I fixed computers and made easy money. And I could always find someone, some tourist, to buy drinks. I spent a lot of time doing that. One day I drank a few hours with a man who said he wanted a personal assistant..."*

Thunder purred from liver-colored clouds. Flashes of light snapped far out to sea, like something broken, beyond repair.

Hugo sat across from me on my bed. Cleaning his sunglasses with the handkerchief he looked me straight in the eyes for a long time, searching for something. I guess he didn't find it, I didn't see any questions in his eyes. He put his sunglasses back on and went out to the terrace.

*"My new employer was much older than me, sold weapons, rented guards he trained himself. He was a fitness freak with a family high up in government. He didn't like hot-heads, told me to cool off, train with the guards in the camp. He said it's easier that way. He liked me. We listened to music, he showed me how to surf, we went fishing, hunting. Sometimes we ran barefoot on the coast, sleeping out with nothing but knives. I kept account books for him, made arrangements. He read Hemingway in English, and asked me about many things, and told me interesting things I found useful later."*

*"One night I told him what I'm telling you now. He said I should stalk her, scare the hell out of her, let her live, in fear, it's better."*

I watched Hugo scan the swollen purple horizon, the yachts, down the beach, up my street, sweeping out past the church to the graveyard at jungle's edge. I tripped on a chair, dizzy from light changes. Hugo was at the far edge of the terrace focused on a small group of people. They were walking out of the jungle, passing through the tombstones on the other side of the church, coming around the back of the church, down the alley past relic stalls and festival booths, stopping to take photographs, picking things up to look at here, talking to a seller there, laughing with each other. But not for long. Hugo whistled, sharp, loud and piercing, like he was calling a dog. Everyone on the street looked up. Tree branches hid my terrace from the woman with huge eyes twisting her head back and forth. Her body melted into a grotesque posture, hung with a swinging flat-white panicked face. She crouched in the shadows of the church where she threw herself against the wall.

**Lyn Lifshin** is a widely-published poet and author of numerous books, including *The Licorice Daughter: My Year with Ruffian* (Texas Review Press); *Another Woman Who Looks Like Me* (Black Sparrow at David Godine); and *Barbaro: Beyond Brokenness* (Texas Review Press). Forthcoming books include *Tsunami as History* (Poetryrepairs.com) and *For the Roses: Poems for Joni Mitchell.*

---

## MOONLIGHT NIGHT: WINTER

*Maxfield Parrish*

December, the
water moves behind
barns, darkly under
snow dunes in
ten thousand hills
pulling moon light
around the
pine trees, a
sound to sleep
and love by
like bells
running thru the
children's sleep
when they dream
of blue sleighs

**Adam Walter** is a native of the Pacific Northwest and lives with his wife and daughter near Seattle. Previous stories have appeared in *Supernatural Tales, Dark Horizons, Fungi,* and the Harrow Press anthology *Day Terrors..*

---

## HIS LAST WRONG TURN

Del, carrying a small plastic bag in one hand, left the cool interior of the Supersaver Food Corral and stepped onto the sidewalk. The noon heat rolled over him as he looked right, past the large, flat Supersaver building and at the sprawling lot where his car was parked, half a block away. Then he looked left to the intersection and beyond, across the street and down a block, at Craigson Grocery. This was an antiquated, two-story building that had probably been there for a hundred years and seemed not to have had a paint job in twenty.

He checked his watch. It was only a few minutes until he was supposed to meet the man.

Suddenly a hubbub broke out in the doorway behind him. Del swung left and headed down the sidewalk. Behind him, and walking in the same direction, a group of men were talking loudly.

A squeaky, thin voice said: "So that damned thing took the business from no less than three guns before it went down. And did it go down, I'm telling you!"

"Who got to take it home then?" said a low, flat voice.

After a pause the first man said: "Now that's something I never heard. But whoever got it woulda had a hell of a job. All that shot in the thing! Anyway, Dusty took the head. That I know—I hang my hat on it every time I'm over there. He's got it right by the front door. Says it's good luck against the snakes. 'Course Dusty wouldn't want me to say, but he has this foot odor problem, and it attracts snakes like you wouldn't believe. Since he put that head up, though, not once has he found a snake in his boots. And it used to be that'd happen, oh, two or three mornings a week."

"That damn Dusty!" This was a third voice, slurred, the man obviously drunk.

"Dusty and his snakes," said a fourth, also drunk. "Say, who ended up with my lighter? You got it?"

"No. Got my own right here."

"Here, wait a minute," said the man with the squeaky voice. The lighter clicked a couple of times, then Del could smell cigarette smoke. "Take it now, Ted."

Del crossed the street at the intersection, then again to the next block, and continued on his way toward the store. The men followed, still talking loudly enough to make Del uncomfortable. With some effort, he kept to his casual pace. Just as he reached Craigson Grocery, two of the men got in front of him, blocking his way to the store's entrance. The next moment, all four men stood facing him.

"All right now, we just want to talk to you a minute," said one, the man with the squeaky voice. He threw down his cigarette and held out an arm, shaking Del's hand. "How do?"

"Hi," Del said.

The men were roughly the age of Del's father, about fifty. They wore whiskers and had graying hair, deeply lined faces, and sun-reddened skin. And each was much shorter than Del. The tallest, the man who had shaken his hand, came up to Del's nose, though his Stetson added several more inches. He was a wiry man but no less imposing than his companions, all of whom were bulky and muscular.

"Yeah, just talk to us a bit." This was the one with the low, flat voice, a barrel-chested man with a crew cut and sunglasses. The man had the jaw flesh of a pit bull. "You're not in a hurry, are you, cowboy?"

Del realized that he himself was the only one not in boots, and the others, apart from the barrel-chested man, wore Stetsons. Was one of these the man he was supposed to meet? He had no way of knowing.

"I am in a hurry, kind of," Del said.

"We ain't gonna take up so much of your time," said the barrel-chested man. "You can spare a couple minutes. *Can't* you?"

"Sure, I don't see why not."

"Fine. Then Carol here has some questions for you." He hooked a thumb to the side, indicating the squeaky-voiced man.

One of the others, this one with a full beard and eyes that hid behind a pair of blurry, thick glasses, said: "Don't make this take all day, Carol. This heat. Damn it!"

Carol had not looked away from Del's face since laying eyes on him. Now he nodded and said, beginning in an ambiguous, cool tone: "Well, okay. How long you been around this town, fella? You ain't a local, or haven't been one long. What part of the country are you from?"

"The West Coast."

"Not a Californian."

"Yes, Northern California. I've been here two months. I'm teaching biology up at the high school."

"Sexual education!" shouted the bearded man, raising his hat to wipe his damp forehead.

"No. I mean not yet, but—"

All four of the men around Del laughed. He felt beads of sweat run down his spine.

"You're getting off the point," Carol said. "That ain't any of our business. Let me just ask you something else here. Where are you headed now? We thought maybe you were going into old man Craigson's place."

"That's right," Del said. "There's a couple things I need."

"What could you be after on a day like this? It's the weekend, fella."

"My wife sent me in to town for groceries, and the Supersaver didn't have it all. Some—ah—some fresh herbs and things. So I thought I'd try here."

Carol snickered, though the three other men now all wore serious, stony faces. Carol said: "It wouldn't be some rosemary you're looking for?"

"Yes. Rosemary, thyme—"

Carol fell into a fit of laughter and bent to prop his hands on his knees, the laugh becoming almost a choking noise. When Carol finally recovered and was looking at him again, Del said: "So you are the guy."

"We're the guys."

The barrel-chested man stepped closer to Del, put two fingers on his shirtfront, and said: "All right, okay. You're going in there and buying us two cases of beer. Weinhard's. That's it."

Before he could think twice, Del said: "That wasn't part of the original—Wasn't what was agreed."

"Listen, cowboy. Itchy Rick. Get moving. Ted, you take him in there."

The one man who hadn't yet said anything to Del stepped forward and led the way into the store. Del followed.

Inside, the store looked like an oversized mini-mart that had moved into a renovated auto repair shop. The place was poorly lit, had dingy concrete floors, and the stock was displayed on simple shelves made of unpainted, yellowed boards. Posters high on the wall above the shelves featured bikinied women, beer, motorcycles, and cattle. One poster, which Del had to look at twice, pictured a six-pack of bottles resting on the seat of a parked Harley, while behind the bike a Holstein bull with beer bottles for horns gazed off camera distractedly.

The skinny teenage boy running the cash register looked up at Ted and Del a moment, then went back to ringing the purchases of two elderly women who were the only other people in the store. Del followed Ted to the register. When the cashier finished with his sale and the women took their bags and left, Ted asked the boy: "The old man around?"

"He was in back, in the stockroom. But he just left. He'll be gone an hour, maybe longer."

Ted nodded. Del suddenly realized that Ted was much drunker than the other men had been. He guided his speech and bodily movements with a tight nervousness, like a man on stilts who has trouble with heights.

"That's all right then," Ted said. "This fella's gonna pay for two cases of Weinhard's, and I'm to take 'em away."

"That so?" the boy asked Del.

Ted slammed a meaty fist down on the counter. "Course it is!"

"Yeah. That's right," Del said and pulled out his wallet. "Two cases."

The boy shrugged, and Del paid for the beer.

"Come along down here now," Ted said.

They set off down one of the center aisles to the back of the store where they turned right and, leaving the main part of the store, entered a low-ceilinged hall. They walked past a pair of restroom doors and came to the foot of some slatted stairs that went up to a narrow, unlit landing.

"We're up the top there," Ted said. "You first."

"Wait," Del said. "I'm not...Maybe this isn't the best idea after all."

"It's as good an idea as it was five minutes ago. Up."

Ted dug a hand into Del's right elbow, then pushed him forward.

At the top Del found a short hall with two doors, both on his left. Del stopped outside the first door.

"Not there," Ted said. "Hell, no. Next one. That's right, now knock."

At the second door Del knocked weakly. A muffled "Come in" issued from the room. Ted opened the door, walked past Del, then waved him in. Del took just two steps inside.

The room was dark and smoky. The blackout shade on the single window was raised less than an inch, letting in just enough light to turn the smoke in the room a hazy gray and give some definition to the surface of things. Along the wall with the window were a dresser and a small bed. On the bed, a few yards from Del, sat a blond woman, her face in profile as she looked toward the window. She held a lit cigarette in one hand and wore nothing but a dark negligee.

"Got somebody to see you," Ted said.

"Is that right?" the woman said, her voice tired but relaxed.

"Says his wife sent him out for rosemary and thyme." Ted let out a laugh that was short but loud, barking. "I say Rosemary's always got time."

"Always," the woman said. She and Ted smiled, both with their mouths slightly open, waiting expectantly on a reaction from Del. After a moment the woman leaned forward, turned on a small lamp atop the dresser, then finally shifted in her spot on the bed and faced them. Del, who hadn't moved since entering the room, took in the woman's face and went completely still, for several moments not even breathing.

Though weak, the lamplight revealed all he'd expected, and more. From the woman's bare shoulders, arms and legs, Del saw that her figure was plump yet not, to his mind, unpleasantly so. Her long neck, though, could not have been much thicker than Del's wrist, and she had the delicate, thin face of a waifish but pretty adolescent. Even her careless expression conveyed immaturity, like that of a girl who might suddenly turn red or burst into laughter at the words "puberty" or "training bra." This contrast between developed body and childish face unnerved Del. It was a discrepancy he could not reconcile.

"Yeah, he was real cloak-and-dagger," Ted said, looking from her to Del. "But, buddy, it's just a small-town trick. The FBI ain't going to come after you for it. Unless of course, you know, they do." He grinned. "Next time, just ask for Rosemary—don't get clever."

Ted grabbed the Supersaver bag from Del and handed it to the woman. She opened it, took a quick look inside, and then smiled at Del. "Perfect," she said. "I have an honest-to-god sweet tooth and can't get anything like these from Craigson."

"Come on," Ted said to Del. "Inside now, inside."

"Yes, come sit here." She patted the bed. Her voice, like her body, was at least twice the age of her face.

After taking a single step forward, Del said: "So there's nothing else...to get started?"

"You bought them their booze or whatever?" she said.

"Yes."

"Yes," Ted echoed and walked to Del. As he passed Del on the way to the door, Ted whispered: "Don't be rude. So her face stopped aging the day she turned twelve. If you stare, it embarrasses her."

"Then that's everything," she said. "Though you might want to shut the door. It's up to you, of course."

Del began to tremble. He raised a hand and wiped the sweat from his brow. Finally he turned and looked away from that delicate, child's face. But Ted was still in the doorway, facing him, and had his hand on the knob.

"Jump to it, cowboy," he said. Then he gave Del an irritated look. "Hell, are you okay?"

"I think I could be sick," Del said, his voice low and weak. "It's the craziest thing, but she makes me feel like a dead man."

"Oh, is that all?" Ted said. He touched his free hand to his Stetson as he pulled at the door. "Wish I could say she gets better from here on."

# Subscribe and Save!

Big Pulp is now available for subscription!
Subscriptions are $40 for 4 issues,
a savings of $2 off the cover price of each issue

Name _____

Address _____

_____

_____

City _____ State _____ Zip _____

*At this time, we are offering subscriptions to
domestic U.S. addressees only*

Start my subscription with:          Fall 2012          Winter 2012

other: _____

Mail to:   Exter Press
PO Box 92
Cumberland, MD 21501-0092

Order online at
http://www.exterpress.com/bigpulp-subscription

Be sure to include the subscription address
and the issue with which you'd like us to start your sub!

Anna Sykora has been an attorney in New York and teacher of English in Germany, where she resides with her patient husband and three enormous cats. To date she has placed 115 tales in the small press or on the web and 248 poems. Writing is her joy...

## HONEY BEE

*Pompeii, August 23, 79 A.D.*

*Lady Fortuna protect me; runaways get flogged...*Tucking her shawl over her head Melissa strode through the empty forum, whose marble columns gleamed sunset-red. Would the Greek sailor be waiting? The pouch under her tunic's breast-band felt like a stone.

The macellum's doors stood open though the stores inside had closed. In the lamplight two youths in coarse tunics were loading a barrow with rotten melons. Two grizzled men—their masters?—sat at a table, nodding over their cups.

No sign of Hector. Her heart sank as she strolled around the central fountain, the young slaves watching her; in a moment they'd ask her what she wanted. She peered into the fish tank near the fountain: only three speckled trout remained.

Should she run home and tell the master she'd slipped out to buy more fish for the Vulcanalia? If she snuck his coins back into the strongbox, he'd never know the difference. The trout peered up at her, hoping for crumbs; they'd missed sacrifice to the god of fire so far. Tomorrow though some cook would chop off their heads with a cleaver. They were slaves.

No, she wouldn't creep home to Rufus Andronicus; she'd run to the river, look for Hector. Fortuna favors the brave.

Rushing out, she almost bumped a ragged hag, cheek marred by a jagged old scar. "*Vale*, my pretty," the woman leered, beady-eyed as a raven. "What, are you running off to your lover?"

Melissa raised her chin. "Hector of Samos has ivy-green eyes. He wears his black hair loose and long."

"I know him." The hag eyed her thick, dark hair, upswept and carefully curled. "I'm Hecuba. Shall I lead you to him?"

"He was supposed to meet me here."

"Plans change," she whispered. "The word's still 'freedom.'"

"I'll follow you then," said Melissa with relief. Just then a tremor rattled the building.

"What did I say?" cried a grizzled drinker. "The gods are angry at Pompeii. That's why the water in the Acqua Augusta tastes like rotten eggs."

"Drink up, you old satyr," the other retorted. "If they're mad, we're their prey."

◊ ◊ ◊ ◊ ◊

"In here." Hecuba pushed Melissa through a tenement doorway that smelled of urine. Inside she fussed with an oil lamp, whose flickering glow revealed painted lovers cavorting in a garden peeling off the walls.

Melissa sat down on the cubicle's only stool. "So when will Hector come and fetch me? He promised to bring me a trunk to hide in."

"As soon as he can slip away from his ship. While we're waiting, won't you have a taste of wine?"

She didn't answer, and Hecuba poured two cups from a pitcher and offered her one. Hesitating, Melissa chose the other; and cackling the hag raised her own wooden cup: "To youth and beauty, and hair well curled."

Melissa took a little sip and choked; clutching her throat, eyes wide open, she collapsed on the gritty floor.

"So age and treachery beat youth and enthusiasm once again." As Hecuba dumped both cups of poison back into her pitcher, another tremor shook the building. Flakes of plaster fell like snow. Peeling off Melissa's white wool shawl, she draped it over the prone girl's face: "No point in spoiling your looks with dust. My Dacians should pay full price."

◊ ◊ ◊ ◊ ◊

"What elegant hair," cooed the villa's pint-size butler. He stroked Melissa's upswept curls, held in place by a dozen stickpins knobbed with real mother-of-pearl. "I've never seen a slave with such a fancy hairdo. She can't be 17."

"Careful, she's waking up." Hecuba counted his silver coins again and thrust them jingling into her own purse. "She has been lucky; her back's unscarred. I checked, and it's smooth as a plum."

"A pity to waste such a choice morsel on foreign savages like these Dacians."

"It's her own fault, for running away." Hecuba hobbled towards the nearest door. "If we took her home to her master, he'd flog her to death...I'll see you again at the Saturnalia festival, old pal."

"If we're still on our feet come December. My sister-in-law dreamed that Vulcan is angry, and that's why he keeps shaking Pompeii."

◊ ◊ ◊ ◊ ◊

Melissa groaned, somebody hammering on her head from inside. She raised her rope-bound hands and touched her hair: yes, she still had the curls she'd shaped, one by one, with the master's curling iron. She wouldn't look like a slave when she reached Rome...

*Good heavens, where am I?* Lights swam in her eyes as she inhaled the tallow smell of pricey candles. She lay on her side in a high, stone bed, in a chamber with a pair of polished brass chairs, the walls all painted with erotic scenes. She'd never seen such acrobats...

"Who are you?" a gruff voice demanded behind her. "Yet another runaway?"

"That's ridiculous." She sat up straight, squaring her slender shoulders. "I'm a free woman. Unbind me at once." Around the bed stepped a paunchy man of middle age, his nose a piggy snout and oiled hair thinning. Instead of a Roman citizen's toga, he wore a fine tunic embroidered with gold, and a jeweled scabbard glittered on his belt.

"Well, why was a free-born lady hanging around the macellum after hours?"

"I was just waiting for a friend."

He grinned, revealing wolf-like canines. "A likely tale. Who's your daddy, little girl?"

"Pericles of Samos, a rich merchant. Tomorrow we're setting sail for Rome."

"And I am the war god, Mars." He pointed at her cheap cork soles. "You wear the sandals of a slave."

"Indeed, sir, I bought them here in Pompeii. They're light and comfy, like walking on air."

He threw back his head and laughed long and hard, his jowls rippling. "And what is your name, you lying slave?"

"Melissa. It means 'honey bee' in Greek. That's the truth."

"Well, I'm Marco Burebista, born in Dacia, and you are invited to our rites tonight. In fact, you're our guest of honor, Melissa. Welcome to the House of the Blood Fountain." Gripping her arm, he pulled her to her feet and out into a garden like a walled alley. Pale pools of light spread from lanterns on poles over ghostly carnations and calla lilies, which smelled sickly sweet as corpses.

"I've heard of a 'House of the Fountain'," she said as he marched her past pear trees studded with unripe fruit, "damaged by an earthquake, sold for a song."

"We bought it for a purpose," he said gaily. "We've grown rich and fat selling honey to the Romans. Now we just want to spoil ourselves." From beyond the high walls, cracked and patched with lighter plaster, shrilled the cries of neighbors celebrating the Vulcanalia: tossing live fish into their bonfires.

*Home with my master, at least I'd know what to expect. If this is freedom—*

"Come on, Melissa." Marco dragged her along. "Our other guests are waiting."

◊ ◊ ◊ ◊ ◊

At the garden's end, three rich-robed dowagers reclined on couches around a fountain, their hair arranged in triple tiers of auburn, fussy braids.

"Here she is," Marco sang out. "Honey Bee—her blood sweet as Dacian honey."

The trio eyed her like circling jackals. "I feel younger already," croaked the most wrinkled, her tall wig sparkling with gold dust. Finger-long fangs glinted at the corners of her crimson-stained mouth.

"My dear Tabiti, what have you been drinking?" Marco inquired.

"We've already downed the savory blood of two choice Libyan goats."

Melissa shed silent tears as the Dacian shackled her ankle to a chain of thumb-long links, fixed to a bracket in the wall. "Let others celebrate the Vulcanalia," he gloated. "We use their ruckus to mask our fun."

"Butler, another round!" Tabiti hit a hand-gong with a clapper, and soon the waters plashing into the fountain's stone basin fell blood-red. Reaching golden goblets, the three crones scooped them full.

One licked the spatters from her palm: "This is delicious, Tabiti."

"But not as sweet as our *honey's* will *be.*"

"Ladies, you really shouldn't kill me and drink me, when I can sing like a nightingale."

"If I want a songbird," croaked Tabiti, "I'll buy one in the forum, in a gilded cage."

"But I can dance like an Egyptian girl."

"And we can hire troupes of Alexandrian dancers."

"But my master had me trained me as an *ornatrice*—he has a thing about hair—and Tabiti, that wig—it's dark as ox-blood—doesn't flatter your pale complexion. I can mix you a henna hair dye to make you look like the goddess Venus."

Snickering, Tabiti shook her head no: "Honey Bee, it's your blood I need." Drawing a curved dagger from his scabbard, Marco tested the edge with his thumb.

Melissa faced him squarely: "And as for you, your bald patch can only spread like leprosy. That's pitiful in a man who still looks potent as a bull in spring, when I can make lettuce poultices to grow fresh hair on your crown like grass."

"Really?" He twirled his dagger.

"Look at me: I'm my own advertisement." Slowly she rolled her head, and her dark curls bobbed like dancing serpents.

"Maybe we should give this ornatrice a chance." He scratched at his bald patch. "We could wait till the Saturnalia, feeding her on honey to sweeten her blood."

Tabiti scowled as if she'd sipped vinegar. "When I was so looking forward to tasting her tonight."

"May I offer you a sample?" asked Melissa, shuddering.

"Don't," Marco muttered in her ear. "She's insatiable, honey; just sit still. Soon we'll get so drunk on imported goats we'll forget about you and fall asleep." With one quick cut of his dagger he parted the rope that bound her wrists. Then he settled down on Tabiti's couch, gave the simpering vampire a hug, and dipped his own golden goblet into the reeking fountain.

Sitting down on the flagstones, Melissa waited for hours, as patient as a slave, while the fountain flowed with crimson blood and the vampires boozed like legionaries. Sometimes they sang off-key songs in Dacian, and though she didn't understand one word, she sat there smiling and hatching a plan, while they guzzled on and slowly grew sated.

Bloated as giant leeches then, they slumped back on their couches and slept, slack mouths dribbling blood. The whole neighborhood had quieted, except for the creak of crickets in the trees and the far-off thrilling of a nightingale.

Melissa drew a stickpin from her hair and started picking at the plaster around the bracket. Maybe a watchdog bigger and stronger than herself had pulled it out? The patch job looked sloppy; some lazy slave had given her a fighting chance.

Marco snored like a horse while she picked and picked and picked, like a bird gone mad, for what felt like a century—as if she were building a pyramid. Freedom, her freedom, felt so near; parched and famished now, she could almost taste it: clear water; water sweeter than honey; water that warms you through like wine...Fiercely she tugged at the crumbling plaster, till her slender fingers bled.

The quarter moon was sailing down the stars when she finally pulled the bracket free. Carrying it, with her iron chain, she tip-toed to the pear tree closest to the wall. Lithe as an alley cat she climbed it, one-armed, and still the bloated vampires slept.

As the high branches bent under her, cracking, she sprang out and grabbed for the wall: *Lady Fortuna, help me!* She dug her fingers in and pulled herself up, loose chain clanking like kitchen pots. Light as a cat she balanced for a breath, and dropped down into the unlit street.

The chain rattled down around her. She held her breath...When nobody shouted, nobody stirred, she thanked the gods for the Vulcanalia: everybody lying drunk in bed. At sunrise they'd come swarming again though, and even if the Dacians didn't pursue her, how could she pass as a free woman, lugging this shackle and chain?

She needed to take shelter...needed to think...Hastening through deserted side streets, she spied a ruined villa in the moonlight, a *Cave Canem* sign on its gate. She rattled the gate—locked, or rusted shut. A doghouse stood in the overgrown garden. No drooling mastiff leaped to attack her.

*Help me again, Fortuna, and I'll offer you a pair of golden scissors...In fact, I'll donate the coins for every tenth head I style to your temple in Rome.* Wrapping her chain around one arm, Melissa clambered over the gate. A rain barrel held precious water, and scooping it out she slaked her thirst. She plucked some hard pears from a twisted tree and devoured them, cores and all. Creeping inside the doghouse then, she pushed aside a petrified dog still shackled to its rusty chain, poor slave.

Night was thinning, but she should be safe for a couple of hours. She had to get rid of her chain somehow, and run and find Hector at the river port. Without any money, though—Hecuba had stripped it— how could she persuade him stow her away?

And Rufus Andronicus would want her back, who loved her; surely he'd post a reward for her capture. Would he flog her to death as a warning to his other dozen slaves?

Maybe he would, but now she'd *rest*. When she shut her eyes new tremors rippled through the ground. Wasn't Vulcan satisfied by all the live fish sacrificed in his honor?

◊ ◊ ◊ ◊ ◊

Melissa heard a rattling overhead, like violent rain. She forced her eyes open, to greyish light. Still dawn? She felt stiff in every limb; she must have slept for hours.

She licked her lips and they tasted dirty. Her hands looked all powdered with fine ashes. They'd wafted in while she was sleeping— ruining her hair, oh woe.

Crawling out she cringed, stung on head and shoulders: pebbles the size of small peas tumbling from the sky! She sheltered under the villa's balcony, and the sinister shower didn't let up. Meanwhile low banks of encroaching cloud made this day dark evening.

*Are the great gods punishing us? Do they want to destroy us all?*

Now a dozen people rushed down the street with bundles; slaves or their masters, she couldn't tell; all shrouded in ashes like Jewish mourners. "To the Stabian Gate!" they shouted. After them a bent old man came cursing, dragging a skinny goat on a rope:

"Don't stand around like a fool," he yelled at Melissa. He didn't seem to notice her chain.

She ran to the villa's gate, and as a panting, plump woman staggered past, carrying a weeping toddler on each hip, Melissa asked: "What's happening, mother?"

"Vesuvius is burning, dear. Run—or get roasted like a pig." Melissa scrambled back over the gate, hauled up her chain and joined the exodus.

At a corner, three youths in coarse tunics were passing bundles into a cellar. "Sister, come inside with us," one cried. "We'll shelter till the gods have spent their wrath."

"No. We should try to escape."

As the streets filled with people cowering under the intermittent hail of stone, Melissa struggled towards the Stabian Gate, which led to the river's port. Just paces ahead, a table-sized boulder slammed into the cornice of a temple, and fragments of gods came crashing down. *Help me, Fortuna—my only hope!*

As black ashes started falling like snow, men with the muscle pack of gladiators came, forcing their passage through the crowd and buffeting her like a child. By now her iron chain felt as heavy as fate. If only she could break it off.

Pompeiians were screaming, weeping, lamenting and calling on all the gods for mercy, while the stones dropped from heaven grew ever larger. Even her breathing hurt. If she only had her shawl, to wrap around her face. Hecuba had stripped that, too...A wooden shutter came clattering down, and she grabbed it and held it up like a shield; and with her other hand she held up her chain, so she wouldn't get entangled—trampled to meat.

Abandoned possessions littered the streets, and men were breaking into a taberna. They handed a barrel out the window...

"Melissa!" cried a familiar, nasal voice, and peering back through the ash-laden air she saw old Rufus Andronicus, smeared and filthy, cradling his strongbox in skinny arms. "Come help me carry this treasure, my dear. I'll forgive you for pilfering 10 gold coins and running away."

As she hesitated, he let the box fall, sank to his knees and clutched his heart. "Why did you leave me?" he bleated as soon as she rushed to his side.

"I heard you tell your brother you'd never set me free, though you promised to 1000 times."

"Help me to a boat, my pet, and I'll do it. I swear by the gods in their majesty."

"Rufus, why should I trust you now?"

"Because I'm dying from this poisoned air."

"Look at this chain: I can hardly walk. How can I help you down to the river?"

Biting his lips, Rufus looked around wildly; and then grabbed the elbow of a short, thick-set man carrying a tool-box: "Break this shackle off her, my good man. I'll give you three bracelets of fine gold."

The good man freed Melissa with a few, sharp strokes, and then turned his hammer and wedge on the strongbox. Rufus called down curses on his head as he scuttled away, loaded down. Coughing, Melissa could hardly see across the street.

"It's the end of the world," Rufus groaned, clutching his weak heart. "And I'm going to die here like a chained dog. You run away; you're young and strong; head for the sea, not the river port. Take all my gold that's left, and hide it well."

She stuffed what she could into her underwear, and then kissed his bald and filthy head, where she'd tried to grow fresh hair for years. "*Vale*, Rufus; you kept your promise."

"*Vale*, my dear Melissa," he choked, and slapped her plump bottom as she skipped away.

Now she wove through the jostling crowds, towards the Marine Gate, which lay farther off. As she staggered down the steep and winding track leading to the sea, she saw just a few boats left below the fishermen's dock and hordes of people scuffling to board them.

"It's Honey Bee!" Turning, Melissa she saw a carved sedan chair descending the slope, carried by four strapping men. "Catch me that slave-girl!" Tabiti croaked. "She belongs to me!" The steep slope bucked like a frightened horse then, and as Melissa slithered downhill she caught a glimpse of Tabiti and her bearers tumbling over a cliff like a handful of thrown toys…

At the dock, burly, black-haired Hector stood on the stern of a ramshackle fishing boat, a boat crammed with wailing refugees.

"We've got no room," he shouted, waving his fist at a hawk-nosed Roman, whose toga bore a senatorial stripe.

"Here I am," cried Melissa hopefully. "I've brought you gold for my passage to Rome."

"How much?" demanded the green-eyed Greek.

"All I could carry, Hector." She pulled a thick golden chain from under her breast-band.

"Men, let's away!" he shouted, snatching it out of her hand. He pushed the pleading senator into the sea and dragged the girl on board. As six sturdy men pulled at their oars then, she heard the bellowing of a maddened bull. Peering into the murky distance, she saw Vesuvius spewing fire…

Gasping for breath, she hugged the boat's side, and then turned her head to watch Pompeii receding: her only home after her father, a freedman—she couldn't remember his face—sold her to Rufus Andronicus, to pay his debts. And she'd never see her poor master again…

All of a sudden Hector caught her from behind and started tearing away her clothes. Plucking out golden cups, ornaments and coins, he tossed them on the deck like rotten fruit.

"Let me be; I'll give you everything!" she screamed. "I just want to live—and work for myself."

Laughing, he dumped her overboard.

"Help me—I can't swim!"

She floundered and sank, just as a tremendous blast of heat seared across the bay. Thrashing to the surface, choking and spluttering, she saw the fishing boat ablaze. A charred body toppled into the sea, still clutching a golden cup.

"Lady Fortuna," Melissa sobbed. "Help me—I don't want to die!" As the fishing boat foundered before her eyes, in the filthy air, the unbearable heat, two small barrels rolled from the deck. She clutched at the nearest and floundering managed to work it under her chest...Bare as a baby in the tumult, now she was floating; could almost breathe.

But strong waves tried to wash her back to shore, as she desperately tried to paddle out, her long hair hanging loose in her face. Oh, she was losing all her precious hairpins...

The whole world grew dark as tar then; and she couldn't see the fire-spewing mountain, whose roaring hurt her ears. Breathing in tiny, terrified bleats, she couldn't see her barrel or the beach. She felt a cooler current though, pulling her along like an invisible hand...

◊ ◊ ◊ ◊ ◊

Many hours later, or maybe days, the skies cleared up again—what a miracle—except for a lingering odor like rotten eggs...Utterly drained, stark naked, and salted like a herring, and thirsty as a battle-battered soldier—but praising Lady Fortuna's mercy—Melissa washed ashore in a cove of white sand...and there, just out of the lap of the waves, she dozed in the sunshine of warm gold.

When she woke, she saw a dusky girl tot with tidy braids, wearing just a woven bib, and peering down, her dark eyes bright, thumb hid in her mouth. Pulling it out, she asked, "Miss, are you a sea nymph?"

"No, but I've survived a terrible storm and the wreck of my merchant ship."

"You have pretty hair. It's so long and shiny."

"Hair is my trade; I'm an *ornatrice*. A free-born *ornatrice*."

That sounded good; that's what she'd tell the people here. Melissa fingered her tresses and smiled. She still had three hairpins to her name.

**Trina Jacobs** was born on Halloween. Her friends say that explains a lot. She left her hometown after college, when she realized that there are places where winter lasts less than six months. She moved to Oklahoma, where she followed her dream of training horses and teaching riding lessons for several years before deciding that a steady paycheck might be nice. Her fiction has appeared in **Big Pulp**, *The Drabbler*, *The Daily Flash 2011*, *Alpha Centauri*, and *I Should Have Stayed in Oz*. She is working on her first novel, an urban fantasy about vampires and werewolves and witches (oh my!). Trina lives near Tulsa, OK with her husband, one horse, one dog, and three cats.

---

# DRAGONS 101

Step 1
1 – Locate dragon.
This could take a while. Don't worry. I'll wait.

Step 2 (or Not)
Have you found a dragon yet?
You haven't, have you?
So why are you even reading this? There's no way we can go to Step 2, yet. Keep looking.
Are you sure you've checked *everywhere*?
Even under the bed? I know you have a lot of stuff under there. Be sure to watch out for killer dust bunnies.
What about the closet? Yeah, that closet. In the back. Yeah, *those* boxes; the ones you've hauled along with you the last 3 times you moved even though you have no clue what's in them.
(Sigh.) How about trying *outside* now? Believe me, if you had a dragon in the house, you'd notice. The sulfurous burps that shake the walls are a dead giveaway.

<u>Step 2 (Really)</u>

Now that you've located a dragon, we will continue.

Stay out its sight so that—

**– *Whooosh!* –**

—it doesn't *set you on fire.*

I see it's too late for that.


<u>Step 2A:</u>

Stop, drop, & roll.

Check yourself into the nearest ER.

We'll continue after you get out of the burn unit.


<u>A Bit of Advice about Dragons</u>

Stop screaming, you know it hurts my ears. Give me that call button! You are *not* going to have security escort me out again. I know you can't put your arms down to your sides, yet. Settle down. We're not going out to find dragons today, we won't be doing that again until all the burns scab over. Okay, *and* the bandages are off. *And* the doctor gives you a medical release. Sheesh.

I just want to give you some information about dragons. Oh, all right, you can press the button for the morphine infusion a few times if you promise to quiet down and listen.

That's better.

'Fire-breathing' dragons don't actually—

Stop laughing.

—breathe fire. If they did, they wouldn't be able to tolerate the nitrogenous atmosphere here on Earth. They would have to live some place where there is fire in the air or where the air is fire. We'd only find them in places like active volcanoes, the sun, or the ninth circle of Hell, which is, of course, absolutely ridiculous.

Really, now. Hysteria is quite unbecoming.

The fire they emit is actually the result of a complex chemical reaction involving sulfur, which is a part of their diet. When sulfur deposits become depleted, dragons have been known to leave eggs sitting out on their kitchen counters for weeks at a time.

'Fire-breathing' dragons have a coating much like Teflon in their intestines and throat. I imagine that's where the idea came. Their tongues are high in asbestos. In the past, before the poisonous residue resulting from the production process was recognized, all asbestos was harvested from dragon tongues. The people who did the harvesting had a really hard time getting insurance. Let's see Mike Rowe take on *that* dirty job.

Anyway, the safest way to approach a 'fire-breathing' dragon is—

Oh, my. Look at the time. Visiting hours are over already. I'll be back later and we'll finish our discussion then.

Nighty-night, don't let the dragons bite.

### The Secret to Approaching a Fire-Breathing Dragon is –
### —DON'T!

What were you thinking? Jumping up and down and waving your arms while shouting, "I found one!" right in front of a dragon is a ***very bad idea!***

It's much, much better to sneak up on them from behind. Of course, they have excellent hearing, so that is a trick in itself.

If you want to catch one, you might try using a very large box held up at one end by a tree truck. Bait it with a virgin of either gender (or is that unicorns?) and call out, "Here, lee-zard, lee-zard." Or something like that.

No! You can't quit! Do you any idea how much trouble I have obtaining apprentices? There aren't any orphans within a hundred miles of here now.

Damn security guards. I should sic a dragon on them. But how will I catch a dragon without ~~bait~~ an apprentice?

John **Hayes** has been published in numerous venues, including *Hungur, Space and Time, Flesh and Blood, Aoife's Kiss, Thema, BareBone, Modern Haiku, Tales of the Talisman, Writers Journal, Premonitions*, and *NFG*. He sculpts, acts and directs in community theater, and once appeared as a scurvy-looking corpse on *Homicide*. Seven of his one-act plays have been produced.

---

## THE WIDOW

Gentle sounds
float across the fields
whisper in her ears
wake her from her doze.
She shakes tingles from her arm
lifts binoculars to her eyes.

In the distant view, a male goat
dances on his hind legs
to the music of a zither
rays glisten on his polished horns.
On break, the workers spoon gruel
accepting of the food and dance.

The music stops
the goat returns to graze.
The foreman snaps his snake whip
workers hasten to their tasks

Mare saddled
she rides across the fields
workers sweat beneath a torrid sun
she tosses a coin between
two random chosen proles.

Battle over, the winner pockets the coin.
The snake whip splits dust laden air
and work resumes.

Inspection finished
she rides to her husband's grave,
removes blue pansies from her saddlebag
drops them on his grave
to wilt in summer heat,
spits on his headstone
"I never believed your lies."

She returns to her veranda
sips cool lemonade.
Her lover's late.
She reaches for her embroidery.

Tim Lieder has been published in *Silverthought, Everyday Fiction, Shock Totem* and **Big Pulp**. Tim also owns and operates Dybbuk Press, through which he's edited and published eight titles including *God Laughs When You Die* by Michael Boatman and *Teddy Bear Cannibal Massacre*. His latest title is a multi-author horror anthology based on the Bible entitled *She Nailed a Stake Through His Head.*.

---

# THE ALBINO DIES

Vincent sat at the bar, drinking cheap vodka from an expensive glass. "Here Comes Santa Claus" played from the jukebox. His white eyebrows dominated his pink eyes. Other patrons avoided him, not because of his condition. Always one or two of them would come up and ask. They avoided him because they knew his reputation.

Vincent knew things. The knowledge had given him an advantage most of his life. He knew which women would fuck him and which friends would betray him. There was a time when he'd use that knowledge, but it always went somewhere else. Finally he took the lessons from Bhagavad Gita and just let his life work.

In fifteen minutes, Sam Lipshitz would walk into the bar, stand behind Vincent and unload a semi-automatic into his skull. Blood would hit the paper Rudolph hanging near the hard liquor. Vincent knew it as much as he knew his social security number and the name of the first girl he fucked. The headlines would read "Albino Dies in Mob Hit." If something happened to Paris Hilton, the headline would read "Albino Dies."

He finished the vodka and ordered a double chocolate martini. He knew it was a woman's drink, but he was curious. Vincent was one of those men who knew things. He knew that the Santa Claus song would end and the next song would be "I Will Survive" followed by Bing Crosby. He would talk to a woman and see the cancer eating her away. He'd have dinner with a business associate and he'd see that man lying bloody in a barber chair. He would walk down the street, bump into a stranger and he'd know how that stranger would die. He'd see the head cracked in the window with the tree breaking the grate. He knew which priests were abusing hookers. He knew which businessmen were stealing. He knew the justifications.

One week ago he saw his fate. It came on as an innocuous tick. He was playing cards with the guys and Sam Lipshitz came up. Now everyone liked Sam. Sam was a good earner, but they held him at arm's length. Tony said that Sam was a little too ambitious. Vincent saw his life in all its hours and minutes. A seat at the bar and a bullet in the skull. Vincent was scared. Didn't talk to Sam all night and when morning came, Vincent looked suitably ruined.

Vincent was expecting the five stages. He went through a hooker and paid for the night expecting to go cry and fuck his way through depression and bargaining. But denial skipped right to acceptance before her mouth was off his cock.

When Sam had started taking out lieutenants, he wasn't surprised. He liked the guys. He went to their funerals. There were nights when he almost called their wives and grandmothers to tell them that they wouldn't be coming home, but the sympathy call never found kindness before the official death notice. He stopped going to the funerals; the snow was too heavy for his shoes.

The next time he saw Sam, he knew where Sam would kill him. He knew the bar. He knew the mirror. He knew the method. He saw the bloody Rudolph. It ruined his day. He passed through all the stages of imminent death in a day. Maybe if he had more time he'd still be in denial. He sent Freddie and Christopher after Sam but they weren't going to help. Christopher crashed his car into an embankment after skidding over ice. Sam just cut them up and sent their pieces through the U.S. Postal system. That sent the entire family after Sam but Vincent didn't have the luxury of hope. He had a bar with a holiday paper decorations, Xmas lights and fake holly.

"You know, Vincent, you don't act like a man whose life is in danger."

"Hi, Sam. How's it going?" replied Vincent. Thirty seconds remained.

"Not so good."

"Me, neither."

Twenty seconds.

"Wanna talk about it?"

"No. Not really." Eleven seconds. Vincent didn't hear the safety because he knew it too well to pay attention.

"You can tell me."

"My wife is starting to worry," said Vincent. "She's been very depressed. The kids are doing fine. Everything seems fine at home, it's just not working. I suppose you could say…"

"Shut up, Vincent."

"Three seconds left."

"Left to what?"

"Your gun's safety is off. Just between us, I don't think you're going to last much longer."

"That's ok," said Sam. Vincent didn't hear another word. The last thing his mind saw was Sam dying as Vincent's men rushed in to save him a second too late. "Here Comes Santa Claus" continued to play in the bloody bar.

A former bank fraud analyst, **Nelson Kingfisher** (not his real name) lives in Austin, Texas (really). His story "Virus" (written under a different name) appeared in the Fall 2011 issue of this magazine. You can reach Nelson, or someone who can find him, at NelsonKingfisher@gmail.com.

---

## CALLER ID

Caller ID has made my job ten times harder. When customers see a toll-free number on their telephone display, they grow immediately suspicious, and their greeting changes from a warm hello to a sharp *"Yeah?"* like the one just flicked at me by a Henry Dranapolis in Winnetka, Illinois. His thumb is poised over the hang-up button, I can tell. I have two words to draw him in.

"Mr. Dranapolis?" I pronounce his name faultlessly, without hesitation, as though the Dranapolises were old family friends. Myself the possessor of a frequently mangled surname, I know that a single misaccented syllable would bring on an instant dial-tone, while careful pronunciation has earned me fifteen seconds of perhaps irrational indulgence.

"That's *Doctor* Dranapolis." His tone of defensive pride suggests that the title represents a doctorate in educational leadership, rather than an actual medical degree. I revise my estimate of our honeymoon from fifteen seconds down to five, then take it back up to ten when I realize his correction suggests a concern for what strangers think of him.

"Dr. Dranapolis, of course. Let me correct that in our records." I check a box on-screen. "Dr. Dranapolis, this is Rob calling on a recorded line from Commerce National Bank."

*"Rob?"* says the doctor. "Give me a break. You think I can't hear through that bullshit TV weatherman accent? What's your real name? Vijay? Sanjay?"

"Raghavendran." I break into my Tamil lilt. "But most Americans prefer something shorter."

"Ragasomething," the doctor says. "Thought so. So you're calling from India."

"Just outside Bangalore, Dr. Dranapolis. You are quite perceptive."

*"Thank you,"* says the doctor, sounding not at all flattered. "And I suppose you're prepared to chat me up with some local news that you read on the *Chicago Tribune* website. Something about the White Sox?"

"Actually," I say, "given your address, north of the city proper, I would presume you follow the Cubs."

"Very *good*, Rags," says the doctor. His voice parodies a first-grade teacher. "That's impressive from halfway around the world. And I *would* be a Cubs fan, I'm sure, if I didn't fucking hate baseball. Most boring game on the planet—except for cricket, of course. No offense."

"Not at all, Dr. Dranapolis. We are aware that the game's charms go unappreciated outside the Commonwealth."

"So we can skip the sports chat. And we can skip the rest, too, as far as I'm concerned. Whatever you're selling, Ragamuffin from Commerce National Bank, the answer is no. No, I am not interested in your high rates on certificates of deposit. Nor am I interested in your low rates on home equity lines of credit. This call, Rags, was over before it began."

"Dr. Dranapolis." I speak rapidly, before he can cut me off. "Let me assure you, sir, this is not a sales call. Sad to say, we have noticed suspicious activity on your credit card."

"Oh." I hear leather squeak as the doctor shifts in his chair. "That's different. Come to think of it, I did think my bill looked a little high."

"I don't believe the item in question would be on your current bill. It is too recent."

"Okay," says Dr. Dranapolis. "I'm hooked. What is it?"

"To begin," I tell him, "I must ask a question to ensure that you are, in fact, Dr. Henry Dranapolis."

"I am, Rags. Come on, you called me."

"I realize that, Dr. Dranapolis. However, you must understand that fraud quite often begins with an unauthorized change to the customer's contact information. What I have called is the telephone associated with your name in our database. Yet it may not be, in fact, your number."

After a moment the doctor says, "Damn." The casters on his chair squeak against the floor. "That's nefarious."

"As you say, sir." The word *nefarious* adds forty points, easily, to his credit score. Perhaps he is a medical doctor after all. "Let me first verify that I am speaking with Dr. Henry M. Dranapolis, of 45 Arborvitae Road, in Winnetka, Illinois."

"Correct."

"Holder of a Commerce National Bank Mastercard, last four digits 6018."

"Let me check." I hear him shuffle through an overstuffed wallet. "That's right."

"Mother's maiden name?"

"Koulpasis."

He spells the name, and I type it in. After waiting a few seconds, I say, "I'm sorry, Dr. Dranapolis. The server is slow today. While we are waiting, let me just correct a common misunderstanding. The person I intended to ask about was the mother of the primary cardholder. Is that the surname you provided?"

After a few more seconds, the doctor says. "Shit. I think the primary's my wife. Kate!" He shouts without covering the mouthpiece. *"Kate!"*

Far off, a woman's voice says, "Just a *minute,* Henry. Jesus."

While we wait, I say, "My computer is back up, sir. And yes, I can confirm that your wife is the primary cardholder."

Feet thump up a carpeted staircase. Kate asks, "What is it?"

"It's the bank. Some kind of suspicious transaction on our card."

"Damn," she says. "I knew this would happen eventually. If you'd let me see the statement once in a while—"

"It's not on the statement. Look, Kate, all I need is your mother's maiden name and I can get it taken care of."

"Okay."

"So what was it?"

"Mom's maiden name?"

"Yeah."

*"Polansky."* I can almost hear Kate's head tilt in exasperation. "Henry, I'm going to need to see the statement this month."

"It's Polansky," the doctor tells me.

"Very good, sir." I type this in. "Now, on August 26, at 11:34 p.m., central time, I show a charge for $54.95 to Temptress-Spankatorium.com. Is this authorized?"

"Um…" The doctor speaks slowly and carefully. "No. It's not authorized."

"What's not authorized?" Kate asks.

"Let me handle it," says Henry.

"Are you absolutely certain, Dr. Dranapolis?" I ask. "The charge is out of pattern, but it is rather small, and there's nothing unusual before or after."

"I'm sure," the doctor says.

"Perhaps Mrs. Dranapolis—"

"Maybe it's something I bought," Kate says. "Or…Damn. Debbie. Debbie!"

A distant teenager shouts, "Just a *minute*, Mom. Jesus."

Dr. Dranapolis lowers his voice. "Let me assure you, Rags. No one in this house would have made that purchase."

"Very good, sir. I will dispute the charge."

"Can we keep it off the bill?"

"I cannot assure that, sir. The item will persist until the dispute is resolved, and that sometimes takes a few weeks."

"Great."

"I'm also going to place the card under heightened surveillance.

Because the transaction is small and isolated, it would be premature to close the account. But often a compromise begins with a small test transaction, so that subsequent charges may be much larger. If anything out of the ordinary happens, your card will shut down automatically. You may wish to carry a second card as a backup."

"Mom." The teenager is closer now. "What's going on?"

"It's the bank," Kate tells her. "Debbie, you know you're only supposed to use the credit card in emergencies."

"I didn't *use* it, Mom."

"Thank you for choosing Commerce National Bank, Dr. Dranapolis," I say. "You have an excellent day, sir." Kate is raising her voice at Debbie when I press END.

I dial another number. During the hold music, I take my headset and laptop out to the balcony. Below me, a tour boat cruises by on the Chicago River, heading toward the Wrigley Building and then out to Lake Michigan. I can't make out what the guide is saying, but the tourists are looking at the apartment block on the far bank—the one we hope to get into eventually—where every residence takes up a full floor and comes with a boat slip in the attached marina.

My fiancée sits on the balcony in shorts and a camisole, drinking club soda and reading the funnies in the Saturday *Trib*. Her name is Clarissa, but online, at least until our wedding, she's known as the Temptress. If you saw her, you'd know why.

"That Indian accent was *awesome*, Rob," she tells me. "I had to slide the door shut so you couldn't hear me laughing. What perv were you talking to this time?"

"Some proctologist up in Wilmette."

"Ooh," she says, "a north shore doctor. Must have one hell of a credit limit."

"I figure thirty, forty grand. Almost all available, I'm sure. That kind pays in full every month."

"How are you going to spend it?"

"I'm going to start with some baseball tickets, maybe boxes at

Wrigley Field. With the Cubs in contention, those should sell pretty quick on CraigsList."

"Save a couple for yourself. Take some time off. You've been working so hard, hon."

"Come on, sweetie. How are we going to pay for that Vera Wang dress?"

"Vera Wang…" Clarissa lowers her eyes demurely. She's had her eye on a backless gown with a long train, but this is the first time we've talked openly of buying it.

The hold music fades, and a customer service rep picks up. "Commerce National Bank. This is Shruti."

"Hi, Shruti. This is Dr. Henry Dranapolis. I've just moved downtown and I'd like to update my phone and address."

"Of course, Dr. Dranapolis," says Shruti. "I'd be happy to do that. May I just verify your mother's maiden name?"

I wink at Clarissa and blow her a kiss. "I think you mean my *wife's* mother."

**D.R. Rice** is a student in the creative writing MFA program at UC Riverside, Palm Desert. She recently retired from a 35-year accidental career in environmental protection and is now writing her first mystery novel.

---

## THE BODY IN THE BASEMENT

I parked near the two-story row house on 46th Avenue. A black and white and the Medical Examiner were already there. A small crowd of neighbors stood in their yards gawking, expressions of morbid fascination and dread on their eager faces.

It was 10:42 and another gray summer morning. The air was wet with the fog that might burn off by mid-afternoon.

I'd been enjoying my Sunday morning routine. Five-mile crack-of-dawn run around Lake Merced, then hit the gym for an hour. The *Chronicle* was divided into neat piles, read now, read later, toss, and I was tucking into my bran cereal with berries, whole wheat toast, trace of butter, when the call came. I dressed quickly, gathered my gear and picked my partner Wendy Hollister up in front of her West Portal home. Her rumpled husband waved from the window, one of their two kids in his arms.

Officers Lamont and Getty had responded to the 911 call. They had quickly surmised it was a probable homicide.

I took the front stairs two at a time.

"Already had your Wheaties I see," Wendy said, as she dragged herself up the stairs behind me.

"Don't knock it," I replied. I opened my sport coat and pounded my taut mid-section with a closed fist.

She grunted and shook her head. Her crumpled overcoat was in need of a trip to the cleaners. One side of her poufy hairdo didn't match the other.

I was still pumped from my morning exertions. Anticipation and curiosity pricked all my senses, made me feel alive and alert, like Superman. A new case always had that effect on me, like the opening scene of a good movie.

Officer Lamont stood guard at the front door. He stepped out onto the welcome mat and filled us in. He nodded towards the living room. We leaned in as he lowered his voice. "The girl who made the call is in there with Getty. She was standing at the open front door when we got here. She led us into the hallway, threw the deadbolt on the door to the basement and pointed down the stairs. Hasn't spoken a word."

The girl was perched tensely on the edge of an ottoman, shoulders hunched, long arms wrapped around her knees, eyes intent on the orange shag. She rocked back and forth like a metronome. The bony length of her curved spine was visible through her shirt. I could have wrapped the fingers of one hand around her scrawny neck. She was a lanky sack of black-clad bones, black jeans, black t-shirt, scratched black polish on her grubby toenails. Another Goth kid. Great.

"Miss, I'm Inspector Lewis. This is Inspector Hollister." I flashed my shield.

No response. I bent down on one knee and tried to make eye contact. Black smudges ringed her green eyes. Unruly red curls framed a small white face. I figured she was in shock, stoned, or both. She could have been anywhere from 13 to early twenties. It was hard to tell with girls.

I nodded to my partner to stay with the girl, figuring that being a woman, she might have better luck getting her to talk. I was anxious to see the body.

The worn wood stairs creaked under my weight. I was conscious of every step, every sound, as I approached the scene, drawn to the dead woman by the bright lights the ME had set up below. There was a handrail along the wall. I was careful not to touch it. The other side was open to the gloomy garage.

I contemplated the woman splayed beside the stairs, one cheek pressed to the cold concrete, an unyielding pillow, arms akimbo. My breath was shallow, an unconscious reaction to the thick odor that rose from the body in the low-ceilinged musty room—sweet and cloying.

The victim wore white wide-legged pants and a pale blue sweater, fuzzy, like angora or something. The straps of her flimsy white sandals had twisted on her ankles, digging into the flesh. The remnants of a broken pearl necklace were strewn on the ground near the body, loose pearls scattered like marbles. There was a congealed brown pool beside the body, its outlines like the continent of South America. The stain around the rent in the back of her cashmere sweater was dark and crusty with dried blood.

I thought about the young girl upstairs. Had she seen the body? Had she stabbed this woman in the back?

The victim's lips were parted, the jaw rigid. Dark hair fell across her forehead and face. Her open eyes were already murky and opaque, arms bent at the elbow, stiff hands and fingers extended, reaching. She wouldn't be telling me what happened.

The Medical Examiner looked up at my approach, nodded a terse greeting.

"How long you think she's been there?" I asked.

"Awhile. I'll know more after the autopsy. Preliminarily, looking at the degree of rigor and skin coloration, at least eight hours, maybe more." With a gloved finger, she drew my attention to the purplish pigmentation on the undersides of the woman's calves.

"Likely cause?" I asked.

"Could be the knife wound though there's also significant head trauma, more than I would expect with a fall from that height." She glanced up at the exposed stairwell. "Looks like the killer may have grabbed her by the hair and smashed her head on the floor a few times for good measure."

"Nice," I said, nodding. I thought of the girl upstairs.

The ME leaned over the body, her short black hair shiny under the lights. Expressionless, with practiced efficient movements, she placed bags over the victim's hands.

I scanned the area around the body. Behind the corpse a small side room jutted out into the garage. The door hung open. A padlock dangled from a metal latch. A small key protruded from the lock. I skirted the body and stepped inside. On one side of the room was a workbench and tools. On the other side, dozens of paintings were stacked against the wall, barely leaving room to walk into the claustrophobic space. Sheets and blankets that might have once covered the canvasses lay crumpled on the floor, ghosts without shape, spotted with flecks of black mold. I stifled a sneeze, pinched my nostrils to prevent another.

Out in the garage, up on blocks, sat the neglected carcass of a classic old Studebaker. There was a drop cloth on the grease-stained concrete beside it as though the mechanic planned to return. But judging by the rat droppings on the soiled cloth, he or she hadn't lifted a tool in awhile.

Behind the car, a side door was ajar. It led into a narrow shaft open to the gray sky above. The airshaft, the width of my outstretched arms, was all that separated the house from its neighbor. Overhead, a lone seagull crossed my line of sight. I walked the length of the corridor. The door at the other end was unlocked. It opened onto the street, at the bottom of the driveway. Up on the sidewalk, two kids peered in the window of the cop car.

The crime technicians had arrived to search for fingerprints and gather evidence. We spoke in soft hushed voices out of unspoken regard for the dead woman and the sanctity of the scene.

I ascended the stairs, stepping over a piece of toast that lay face down on the kitchen floor. A smear of dark jelly marred the black and white linoleum. The counter was littered with drinking glasses, crumbs, a plastic sack of bread, a butter-smeared knife and an open jar of jelly. There was butter inside the jar, contaminating the glossy fruit spread. My first wife used to do that. Irritating as hell. I shook my head in disgust.

Beyond the window over the sink, across the airshaft, a shadow shifted in the house next door. Someone had darted from my field of vision like a startled fish swimming to the other side of the bowl.

In the living room, my partner spoke in a gentle murmur, trying to coax information from Goth girl.

"I'm sorry," the girl muttered. She hiccupped and sobbed in spasmodic bursts, fighting to catch her breath, like a child that's been crying so long it can't stop.

"What are you sorry for, sweetie?" Hollister asked.

No response from the gasping girl.

An unadorned black book, the size of a slim paperback, lay on the counter beside a well-used aluminum toaster. I picked it up. It flopped open where a pen was inserted between the pages. A dense loopy scrawl filled the front half of the book. A diary. My eyes found the most recent entry, dated July 14, the previous day.

*Hate you, hate you, HATE you! Wish you were dead. Feed you to the lions. In their throats, wooly with matted fur, their roars grow louder, closer. Their cell walls rattle and shake. The Lion House echoes with their hunger. They shake their massive heads, beads of spittle fly, impatient for the slab of red meat. Like I wait, for the end.*

On the front inside cover, a name, Julianne Lazar, and the words *Tales from the Zoo that is my Life*. January 1983. Nasty bit of creative writing, I thought.

I moved back into the living room to have another look at the girl. She twisted to look over her shoulder at me.

The girl sprang up and covered the ten feet between us before I realized she had left her seat. She lunged for the black book, snarling like an animal, a desperate guttural sound from somewhere deep inside her.

"Oh, is this yours?" I asked, holding the book just out of reach above my head.

Her eyes widened, pupils dilated like black shirt buttons. She was tall, close to six foot but not very strong. Still, I staggered back a step as she flailed at me with singular focus, her eyes locked on the black book.

My partner and Officer Lamont each grabbed an arm. Wendy handcuffed the girl's bony wrists. She howled one last time, tears and snot flowing, before she collapsed, first to her knees, then all the way down. She curled on the floor, chest heaving, eyes clenched shut.

They dragged the girl to the patrol car for the ride to juvenile hall. After that sudden outburst, she was lifeless as a rag doll. Hopefully, Dr. Moon would get her talking.

Lamont's partner had talked to the neighbors. The girl, Julianne, was sixteen. It was just the mother and daughter who lived in the house. No one had heard or seen anything unusual the previous night.

The lookie loos out on the sidewalk craned to see what they could see as the bagged body was moved to the waiting coroner's van.

I sighed. Nine times out of ten it was a family member. Was it as simple as that? Had Goth girl stabbed her mother in the back, then shut and locked the door, leaving her mother for dead overnight on the cold, cracked concrete? I was glad I didn't have kids.

Coy Hall lives and writes in Kentucky. His published stories span a range of genres, including horror, sci-fi, adventure, western, fantasy, and crime. Reach him at coyhallfiction@yahoo.com.

## THE FIVE AND DIME SINNERS

The kids were whispering about it when the homeroom bell rang. Dirk Fannin, seventeen, had three hostages at Mick Bryant's nickel and dime store. The cops had caught up with him after he'd knocked over the Blitz Valley Savings and Loan. He'd ducked into Mick's place and flashed a .38. The Sheriff and his deputies were outside the store in the parking lot trying to talk Dirk down. It was big news and there wasn't a hushed voice in Blitz Valley High till everyone had heard about it and talked big about the outcome. The kids who liked Dirk said he'd come out on top with a sack of money and an open road. Most of the kids said he'd come out in a body bag with enough metal in his body to attract a community of miners.

Unlike the other kids, Meg Masters didn't want to talk about it. She thought about it plenty, though. Dirk was her man. And though she tried not to let on, she was mad as hell that he hadn't let her in on this one. I bet he wishes he had, she thought. She wasn't a slouch with a pistol. Sure, she was sixteen. But her daddy had taken her on trips to shoot rabbits when she was only eight. His mistake.

The bell rang. The kids around Meg stood and moved out into the hallway. A river of bodies passed by the class door, chattering. Meg clicked her nails against the desk.

"Miss Masters?" Mr. Hunt, twenty-eight, social studies, tall, chubby, fleshy, round face, leaned his backside against his desk. He crossed his legs first, then his arms. He wore a sweater with a tie underneath. He had thick glasses.

Meg looked up. "Yeah?"

"You have a class, I assume?"

"What gave you that idea?"

"Cut it out. Get up and go."

Meg took out a couple pieces of bubble gum. She tossed the wrappers on the floor and bit down on the gum.

Hunt kept his arms crossed and looked at the wrappers.

Meg got to her feet. She wore a plaid skirt, light sweater, saddle shoes. She had light brown hair and brown eyes that hid beneath long, naturally curling lashes. She chomped down her the gum as she walked forward. She sneered at Hunt.

"Say," he said, "you're close with that boy Dirk, aren't you?"

Meg watched him. She knew the look on his face. It was the look men get when they realize, if only slightly and for a second, that they can't stand women. Everybody guessed Hunt was a fairy, with him not being married and all. But his look said otherwise. There was frustration in it. "Sure," she said; and smacked the gum.

"I'd say you're awfully worried. Probably just dyin' to get outta here. I'd be worried, too. If I'm not mistaken ol' Sheriff Hadley's had some words with that boy before. And I'd say…"

Meg turned and walked off.

Hunt laughed as she hit the door. Then he said, "You either go pick those wrappers off the floor, girl, or I'll see you stay after for detention. I'll put an eye on you for the rest of the day."

If I ever killed a man, it'd be one like you, she thought. But Dirk needed her now. She couldn't argue. She stepped down the aisle of desks and picked up the wrappers. She stuffed them in her purse.

"Thank you, Miss Masters," Hunt said.

"Don't mention it." Meg hurried off before the frustrated man could open his mouth again.

Hallway traffic was light. A few kids chatted at their lockers. Some of them, like Meg, wouldn't make it to class. The bell rang. Damn, Meg thought. McQueen, the principal, would be out and about now. She hurried down the hall. The front doors were too tricky, so she headed for the usual skipping route. The janitor/maintenance room had an unlocked door that led to the trash bins out back. From there you had to scale a wood fence. It wasn't tough.

Meg stopped dead at the restrooms when the girls' door opened outward. Jen Powers, thank God, stepped out. "What're you still doin' here?" Jen asked. A short, stick-thin redhead, Jen never wore anything but slacks. She wore a coat over her blouse. Either she'd left the restroom on fire or she'd just grabbed a nice, long smoke. "I figured you'd bust out for Dirk."

Meg liked Jen. She understood her. They thought alike, fought alike, and talked alike. And unless they both fell for the same man, they'd remain friends. "That's where I'm headin'. Wanna come?"

"Hadley and his boys are in the parking lot. What can we do?"

"I'm gonna make 'em make a decision," Meg said. She had the plan in her mind. All she needed was a gun. And a ride. "You got your brother's car with you?"

Jen smiled. Her lipstick was the only thing brighter than her hair.

The two girls rushed down the hallway and out through the usual escape route.

◊ ◊ ◊ ◊ ◊

Dirk Fannin had a seat behind the cash register, away from any windows. He was a short kid, 5'7" on a good day, but he was made hard. He wore his black hair shaved on the side and longer on top. It was slicked greasy and combed backwards. He wore ripped jeans and black boots. A white t-shirt clung to his strong shoulders. He had his hand on a glistening .38. A bag of money with Blitz Valley written across the front waited on the counter.

Old Mick Bryant sat on the floor with his cashier, Wilma Marcum and a customer, Tracy Hendershot. Bryant was in his seventies; he wore a black toupee and had his horseshoe haircut dyed, somehow, one shade darker than the top. He was an arrogant man and cantankerous. Wilma, the cashier, was married with three kids. She'd said that at least fifteen times. In her forties, she was too modest to let anything but the tips of her ears show uncovered. She wore clunky, ugly brown shoes that had gone out of style when Eisenhower took office. Those are Roosevelt shoes, Dirk had told her. But she didn't get it. Tracy Hendershot was in her late twenties; pretty, blonde hair. She'd stopped in on her way to work to pick up some medicine for a headache. Her car had stayed running out in the parking lot until Dirk gave the okay for the cops to shut it off.

"Hey Blondie, you keep a man company?" Dirk asked. He grinned. He had ideas about taking Blondie along for the ride. They could use her car if there was any gas left in it.

"A man maybe, but that don't include you," Tracy said. She sat with her back against the wall. All four of them were behind the counter.

Dirk looked up at the shelves. "You sell Grape Nuts for a nickel or a dime?" he asked.

"They're twenty cents," Wilma said.

Dirk whistled. "Rip-off, old man. And say Blondie, I think this makes me a man anywhere and everywhere." He held up the gun and laughed.

"You're nothin' but a punk," Mick said. "A two-bit thief."

"Gramps, you die first, understand? Now shut it, I was talkin' to Blondie. Now you gonna come over here or I gotta make ya?"

Tracy shook her head.

"Aww, come on girl, I won't violate ya. Not too bad."

Wilma, for a reason Dirk couldn't guess, started to cry. She hid her face in her hands and her shoulders heaved. Mick patted her back.

"Baby, you ain't got nothin' to worry about!" Dirk said. He laughed and tapped the pistol against his leg. "Damn all you, you square-ass bluenoses. I gotta a girl waitin' anyway." He crossed his arms and let his finger slide back and forth across the trigger.

"Lucky her," Tracy said.

"Yeah, she'll be lucky if Hadley and his cronies don't pinch me. Offers on the table, though, gal. You can be my girl if you like the look of all that green. Or you can marry a dull polo shirt and play bridge for kicks. You imagine that kinda life? Hey, Wilma, why don't you tell us how fun it is? Livin' like that."

Wilma kept crying.

Tracy shook her head.

Dumb, Dirk thought. He stared up at the Grape Nuts again. The Sheriff had been quiet too long and that bothered him a little. What's he got up his sleeve? Dirk thought. Nothing he can do, though. This is a stalemate. Who breaks first? That's the way it'll be played. Straight and simple. They die or I go. Not a hard decision unless you're a man with pride. Hadley had that. Plenty of it. Dirk tapped his foot. Talk damn it, he thought. Get on the horn and give me a choice.

"Worried?" Mick asked.

"You're dumb, aren't you?" Dirk pointed his gun. Tracy and Wilma jumped away. Mick played tough-guy and straightened his back. "Not unless they make me, dad," Dirk said. "Or if you really make me. I, for one, ain't dumb. Back to the wall, girls." He motioned with the gun.

Sheriff Hadley's voice came through the front window. "We're not movin' out, sonny. Why don't you just let them folks go?" Obviously, he too, had grown tired of the silence.

"Well, you better play your card if ya got one," Dirk shouted. "I go or they die. You decide." Then to the three on the floor, "Easy, ain't it?"

Hadley was quiet for a moment. "Come here, Dwayne," he said. Dirk couldn't hear him after that.

◊ ◊ ◊ ◊ ◊

Meg had two places in mind. First, her daddy kept a revolver in his dresser, in the second drawer down, behind the socks. He was at work, so that wasn't a problem. Her mother had died when she was born. The house would be empty.

The boxed and weathered single story was quiet when Jen pulled her brother's car up to the curb. Old Mrs. Blagg walked with a parcel held against her chest up the sidewalk. She didn't look at the two girls. The sound of a radio voice drifted in the air from an open window. They're probably all over Dirk's case, Meg thought. Everybody's glued to a radio right now.

Jen waited in the car and left it running. Time, after all, wasn't on Dirk's side.

"Be right back," Meg said. She slammed the door and ran up the sidewalk. She had her keys out when she reached the door. Meg rushed through the living room and into her father's bedroom. The bed was unmade and three sets of clothes lay wadded on the floor. The room smelled funny. The morning sun shone in bars through the blind. Meg got the gun, checked it out: six bullets; clean; safety on. She stuffed it in her purse and rejoined Jen in the car.

"Got it?" Jen asked.

Meg nodded. "Hit the gas. I'll light up anyone dumb enough to stop us."

Jen pulled out from the curb and mashed the pedal. The car roared up the street, drawing plenty of attention. Nobody tried to stop them.

The second place Meg had in mind was Blitz Valley High. Jen pulled into the front parking lot, a couple rows back from the front entrance. A stiff breeze came through the passenger side window. Meg pulled the gun from her purse and showed Jen.

"You plan on usin' it?" Jen asked.

She's scared, Meg thought. But no wonder, I'm scared. And she's got nothing pushing her into this. Except me. "No," Meg said. "But why don't you beat it, huh? I'll go in and take the brunt of it. You get home."

Jen's eyes were pleased with the suggestion. She tried not to show it. "But say, Meg, I don't want ya to think I'm scared. It's just…"

"I get it," Meg said. "You helped enough." Meg let the gun drop back into her purse. She opened the door and got out.

"Give 'em hell," Jen said.

Meg closed the door and turned towards the school. Jen took off. Meg felt her nerves in her stomach and chest. Her mind pounded and the thought of the gun sickened her for a second. But it was either Dirk or her. And they're easier on girls. Even when they have guns. I can do anything I want right now, she thought. The idea lingered.

Meg moved between the rows of cars, watching her reflection in the windows as she passed. The sun burned in the sky, warm for early autumn. Freshly dead leaves blew on the wind from a playground across the street. I'm going to do this big, Meg thought. Her hair flipped in the breeze.

Nobody was at the door to greet her. The bell for second period wouldn't ring for another fifteen minutes. Mr. Hunt, for one, wouldn't have a class till then. Meg made up her mind and started down the hallway. Hunt's classroom was empty. Meg bit her lip, thinking. The teachers' lounge. She turned back up the hallway and walked to a doorway that forbade the entry of students. They'll make an exception, she thought. Meg turned the knob and went inside. Hunt, along with two other teachers, Mr. Gable and Mr. Frost, sat at a table drinking coffee. Their laughter stopped when Meg entered the room. Hunt took the lead. "Miss Masters, are you just begging for trouble today?" The look she hated dominated his face.

Meg pulled the gun. "Just take it easy, fellahs," she said. She showed the revolver off, silver plating and pearl handle. She thought about spinning the cylinder but didn't want to take the chance. She pointed it instead.

The three teachers lost their manhood and recoiled. "Now…now," Hunt started. His chin quivered.

"I'm gonna tell you once to shut your fat face, Hunt. Once. I'm not soft. You understand? Frost?"

Frost nodded.

"Gable?"

Gable nodded.

Meg moved to the back wall of the lounge. She didn't want anybody coming up behind her. She dropped her purse to the ground. The gun felt heavy in her hands. A clock ticked on the wall and each second echoed the room was so silent. Finally, Meg said, "Gable, go and get Principal McQueen. You tell him Hunt dies first if he plays games. I wanna talk."

Gable, a math teacher in his forties with gray hair at his temples, stood and backed toward the doorway. He felt for the handle blindly, then stepped out and disappeared. The door slammed shut.

Frost, another math teacher, in his twenties like Hunt, skinny, bald, no glasses, clean shaven, said, "Meg, listen. We realize you're under stress. What with the news and all. But put the gun down. It's not gonna solve anything." He dropped his chin and raised his eyes. "Think about it."

"It's gonna solve plenty," Meg said. "Where the hell is McQueen? Gable better not be playin' games. I'm not."

Hunt closed his eyes and said a prayer.

"I like this side of you," Meg said. She watched him.

He played deaf and dumb and kept talking to God.

"Please, Meg," Frost went on.

"Shut it," Meg said. She took out her gum and threw it at Hunt. The pink glob bounced off his chest, hit his leg, and fell to the floor. He didn't react. "You better hope McQueen gets here soon," she said. Just hold on Dirk, she thought.

McQueen stuck his head through the door. His eyes were as big as ping-pong balls when he saw the gun; like he hadn't believed what Gable had told him. "Miss Masters?" he said. McQueen was in his fifties, a tall, broad-shouldered man, flat-top haircut, gray. He looked like the military had eaten up most of his life. He stood straight and brushed at the front of his suit when he entered the room. "What is this?" he asked. He wanted to lash out but had enough discipline to fence it in.

"Two things," Meg said. She held the revolver on Hunt. "You get the Sheriff on the line. Either he comes out here and lets Dirk Fannin get out of that store and on his way or I kill these two."

"But…"

"Second," Meg said. "When I know Dirk's away, I'll hand this over and go quietly. Move."

McQueen opened his mouth to speak. The wheels of his brain turned over and he thought better of it. He nodded.

"Oh, yeah," Meg said. "And tell the kids to split. Get 'em outta here."

"Right away," McQueen said. He left the room.

Seeing big, bad McQueen bow down and submit to her word got

Meg off. She liked the feeling. It was a high that staved off any fear she had about the outcome of things. Dirk will get away and he'll know it's me behind it. He'll stay with me for good now. She felt like a real gun moll, just like in movies. She almost felt good enough to pull the trigger.

"You won't hurt us?" Hunt asked.

"You're a real tough guy, aren't you? Whatta ya say we play a game, creep?" Meg laughed and told the teachers to get on the ground.

◊ ◊ ◊ ◊ ◊

Dirk told Tracy and Wilma to step back. "Don't wanna get blood on those clothes," he said. "Except you," he told Wilma. "You need an excuse for a new set."

Mick was on his knees like he was told. His fire died and he didn't want to fight anymore.

"Get back!" Dirk shouted.

Tracy and Wilma stood and backed off.

Dirk got out of his chair and held the gun out.

"I'm sorry, son," Mick said in a quivering voice. "I take it all back."

"Is that right, dad? Just like that?"

Mick nodded.

"Please don't," Wilma said. "He was just mad. He didn't mean it."

Dirk touched the gun to Mick's temple. The cold steel made the old man jump. You guys ain't got a lick of sense, Dirk thought. Think I'm going to kill you all when I'm this close to getting out? But they weren't the gambling kind. They played it cool till things were on the line. Then they backed up and begged. Most people are that way, Dirk thought. Just about everybody. He pushed Mick's head back and forth with the gun. "Tell ya what," he said. "If Blondie agrees to give me a ride, then I'll forgive ya."

"I'm sorry, Tracy," Mick said.

"Not sorry enough to disagree, though" Dirk said. "Not by a mile. So what'll be, babe? You wanna see his brains or you wanna tag along? I won't be rough with ya." He smiled.

"I'll go," Tracy said. She stared at the ground. The words were dry and stiff and lifeless. Her face was white.

Sheriff Hadley's voice came through the window. "Sonny, can I step in if you see I'm unarmed? Just to talk?"

"Sure, dad, join the fun," Dirk shouted. He stepped away from Mick and turned toward the front door.

Mick let out a shuddery breath and dropped back against the shelves. The boxes and cans shook a little.

Hadley, overweight, short, wearing a heavy mustache and tan uniform, came through the door and a little bell rang. The sheriff held up his hands, empty. He pulled his pockets out, nothing.

"Fine," Dirk said. "Just keep your hands high. Spill it."

"I'll tell it to you like it was told to me. There's a girl at the high school says she'll kill two teachers if we don't let you outta here without interference. Understand?"

Meg, Dirk thought. Hot damn. Girl's got drive.

"We're goin' up to the high school now. My guys and the state boys. We're headin' out. You gotta leave these folks alone, though. That's our end of the deal."

"Sure," Dirk said. "I'll play nice."

"Fine, then. You head out."

"Sure, dad. But, say, how much of a head start do I get?"

"Two hours."

"Swell. Now don't let the door hit ya in the ass, gran'ma."

Hadley nodded. He backed to the door, still holding his hands up. The bell rang and he was gone.

"That your girl at the high school?" Tracy asked.

Hadley, his deputies, and the state police left the parking lot in a flash, sirens blaring.

Dirk shot a glance at a clock on the wall and then grabbed his money off the counter. "She's nothin'," he said. "You're my girl, now. Remember? Let's split, Blondie."

Tracy left Mick's nickel and dime at gunpoint. Her car had plenty of gas. Dirk drove.

**Dylan Gilbert's** fiction has appeared in *Slow Trains, Pearl, The Westchester Review, Blood Moon Rising,* and *Word Riot,* among others. He lives with his wife and son in New York's Hudson Valley. He can be found online at http://dylansstories.weebly.com/.

## RETURN TO NATURE

### 1

I keep breathing a musky scent, dark and swampy, mixed with the pine floor, the rubber mat, the residue of burned incense. Then the musk overpowers them all, pulling levers in my brain.

I push into Downward Dog, breathing deeply, the world around me—the other yoga students, the teacher's voice, the New Age music—all slowed down and heightened.

From Down Dog I lower to Plank position, then Chaturanga. Rising into Cobra, I see her toward the front: thick thighs, ruddy cheeks, damp black hair. She's ovulating. I know, though I don't understand how. I've had these strange sensations since the retreat last weekend.

I twist into Right Angle and notice a man, wiry with thinning curly hair, wearing a peach-colored tank top and tights, gazing upward with mock serenity. Edward Berkel, the weasel, a friend of my wife who was a wart on my knuckle at best before she moved out, but now that she's gone, I've grown to despise him. The bastard even helped her move out of our house.

I was supposed to stay away for the day, so I hung out at my friend Gus's, but my mind was playing out every possible angle to stop this choice of hers. But I had used them all. I'd been begging, pleading, reasoning, wooing, threatening and catastrophizing for six weeks already, but she would have none of it. And there I was, sitting in front of a stupid baseball game on TV with Gus and his family, knowing a half mile down the street my life was being ripped away.

I bolted up and stormed to my car, Gus in pursuit. "Dude, come back." But I was already starting the engine. "Dale, don't go there. You'll just cause yourself more pain," he said, hustling down the steps. I drove away, leaving Gus on the curb, and headed to the house.

I pulled into the driveway and *his* car was there, Berkel's beige Prius. Why the hell's he here? I thought. I drove off, circled around the block and passed by the house again. I repeated this for twenty minutes till I saw her bringing down a box overflowing with CDs, *our* CDs. She looked tired, pale, strands of sweaty hair pasted on her forehead. I pulled up the driveway and jumped out. She rolled her eyes and glanced back toward the house. "You promised," she said, barely above a whisper.

I stepped up to her, took the box from her hands, laid it on the ground and embraced her, my chest heaving, animal-like noises vibrating in my throat, my head on her shoulder, tears soaking into her shirt. I felt a single hand on my back. "It's going to be okay, Dale."

I sobbed more violently and clung tighter.

"Okay, Dale, I have to go. We'll talk."

I kept squeezing, trying to keep her with me. "I can't. I can't."

I felt strong hands on my shoulders pulling me away. It was Gus. Jenna's sister and Berkel were standing on the steps watching the spectacle, boxes at their feet. Gus turned me away from them and, holding my shoulders close to his body, walked me to his car. I glanced back and saw Berkel leading Jenna into the house, *our* house. A flash of adrenaline shot through me and I started to charge him, but Gus restrained me with his bear-like arms and hauled me to his car, telling me we'd come back for my Buick that night.

I sat in the passenger seat, my heart pounding in my ears. I was going to snatch him by the throat and beat the shit out of him. But I don't do that to people. I grew up with that cowboy shit, dad smacking us whenever we were "out of line," but I never took that road, rarely even raised my voice at people. I looked to Gus, whose somber gaze was on the road. "Gus, I don't know what happened. I was going bash his head in."

"It's a normal reaction. You're devastated and this asshole wants to play the hero or something."

"No, you know that's not me. I'm a damn pacifist."

"But it's in us, you know? Primal rage."

"No, it's not in me."

About a week after this drama, I started bumping into Berkel at my drop-in yoga classes. And it's bad enough I have to see him, but on top of that, he's always coming up to me after class like some know-it-all, talking to me about the right way to do yoga. One time I came in late by two minutes because of traffic, and he approached me afterward to tell me entering late ruins the class energy.

As we start on Sun Salutations, I push him out of my mind, refusing to let him ruin my experience. I'm flowing through the asanas when I sense something in front of me, a being, sentient, not whole though. The yoga teacher, the slim blond, she's pregnant. I wonder if she knows. But how do *I* know?

Moving into headstand I glide up effortlessly, my head and elbows rooted to the floor, my feet rising toward the sky. I feel strong today. Usually I can barely get up. Then I hear a nasal voice: "Excuse me, can we turn the music off? It's disturbing my concentration." *Him.* Berkel. I wobble, lose my balance and come down to my feet. "Maybe we could vote on it," Berkel suggests.

We lay in Corpse pose, final relaxation. I feel my limbs heavy and relaxed, the energy from the exercise flowing through my body, but there's a strange whistling sound distracting me. What the hell is that? Maybe a squeaky machine in the basement? A car alarm going off up the block? I try to put it out of my mind, but it's torturous. I open my eyes and glance toward the sound and it's *him* again: legs draped over a bolster, body covered with a blanket, an eye pillow blocking out the world, a nose whistle that would make a dog howl.

I can't take this shit. I grab my gear and head out. Parked behind me, too close, is a little beige Prius—*his.* The same one he used to help Jenna move out. I look in the window and picture it full of our belongings.

I touch the door handle, not quite knowing why, and sense his hand print. I feel a tingling in my bladder and the shaft of my penis. I pull it out and its plump, healthy, like when I was 19 or 20. A stream of golden piss gushes onto his door handle, splattering back at me and dripping down the door.

I get in my old Buick and put it in reverse, and, without thinking, slam the gas and smash into his Prius. I pull away, splintered plastic crunching under my wheels. I begin to snort and giggle as I picture him putting his hand on the wet door handle and then bringing it up to his nose and sniffing.

But as I get closer to home, the excitement of my deed starts to wear off. What was I thinking? I worry that I was seen. Maybe I should get in touch with Berkel and tell him, say it was an accident and I was in a rush, but offer to pay. But what about the piss? And I can only imagine his saccharine lecture. Plus, he'd tell Jenna.

I pull up my driveway and as soon as I see the faded gray steps, the bushy Elm and the green mail box with Dale and Jenna Glass written on it, I get the image of her leaving, standing with the box of CD's in her arms. I live that moment of her leaving every day when I come home. Sometimes when the images are too cruel and the regrets and should-haves too loud, when it takes Herculean effort just to eat or even move, I stay at Gus's. This may be one of those nights.

I kick off my shoes, peel off my shirt and go to the backyard, a quiet place to sit and think, but there's something out there. A huge buck, wide antlers, thick-chest, not twenty feet off, eating my garden like it was his very own. He lifts his head in alarm, and we lock eyes. He lopes around and leaps over the fence.

"You bastard!" I roar, flying out of my back door in my bare feet and shorts. I hoist myself over the fence, clearing it easily, and take off behind him. He weaves through the bushes and into the street behind my house. I plow through the brush, keeping sight of the brown rump, now moving into the woods. I'm on him, leaping logs, ducking branches, my toes gripping and tearing at the earth with each stride.

He starts up a slope, but I'm closing in, using my hands to scramble up the hill. He disappears over the plateau and as I reach for the edge, a stone gives way under my foot. I slam to the ground and skid down on my belly, fingers clutching at the loose earth till I slide to a stop. Dirt and leaves stick to my sweaty torso and face, my breathing is fast and labored. I sit on the ground, elbows resting on my knees, and allow my breath to slow down. What the hell am I doing?

I brush myself off and notice my knees and arms are scraped and bloody. I trudge home. A neighbor, the old guy who lives behind me, is out on his back deck, watching me. I nod like everything's cool. Yeah, I always go out in my bare feet covered in blood and muck.

I run hot water into a tub and fill it almost to the rim. I climb in and every raw spot of skin screams out as it makes contact with the soapy water. The pain eases and I lean back, watching a slice of moon rise through the bathroom window. I gaze at it, glowing and ancient, and feel the power of it in my chest. My muscles twitch and my breath slows down and deepens. I feel writhing and twisting in my belly. I'm ravenous.

I slog out of the tub to my fridge, standing wet naked, a puddle forming at my feet. I pull out a plate of rice and beans, sniff it and lay it on the counter. I wade through yogurt, peanut butter, mayonnaise, cheese, lettuce. I want fucking meat!

◊ ◊ ◊ ◊ ◊

I march toward the back of the market through the cereal aisle, boxes whizzing by in a blur, till I get to the meat section. I grab at the packaged cuts of beef, feeling the weight and tossing them aside till I find a fat red steak. I snatch it and head to the counter, but a few steps off I freeze, panicked it may not be enough to fill me. I go back and grab two more.

Clutching the steaks to my chest, I drop them on the black conveyor belt. The clerk looks startled when she sees me. She quickly bags the meat, keeping her eyes on me the whole time.

I screech around every turn to get to my house. Once in the

driveway I grab the bag of steaks and run up the stairs. I throw my three pans, the ones Jenna left me, on the stove and pour oil in them. I rip off the plastic from all three steaks and drop them in the pans. They start to crackle and hiss, just a hint, and the smell makes my heart pound. I dip my finger in the beefy grease and suck. It burns, but I do it again. I snatch the steak out of the pan and bite into it, ripping off a shred of meat, only barely cooked on the bottom. Chewing the sinewy fiber, I swallow a large clump. Then, clutching the steak in both hands, I rip off hunks with my teeth, juice flowing down my chin, straining to force the thick lumps down my throat.

Once finished I flip the other two steaks and when they're lightly brown on both sides, I devour them too. Halfway through the second I stop, let out a long uneven burp and shove the half-eaten steak aside. My head feels airy, my eyelids suddenly heavy.

I go into my bedroom and see a strange man. I jump back and shout, but then realize it's my mirror. The two days of scruff on my cheeks is smeared in grease and steak juice. My brows are bushy, my eyes glazed and wild. I look like a drug addict or a survivor lost at sea.

I edge my hip on the bed, lean back, and all is black.

2

I hear a dinging in my dream, over and over, till I realize it's my doorbell. I pull myself out of the darkness of sleep and stagger to the door. I open it and see Gus, hair wild, belly hanging over his bike shorts. "Dude, what's wrong with you?" he says.

"I don't know," I say, stepping inside, followed by Gus.

"You look sick or something."

I notice the pans on the stove, the meat juice on the counter. My memory starts to trickle back, then flood. I sit. "Gus, something's wrong with me."

He puts a hand on my shoulder. "What's going on, buddy?"

"You know Jenna's friend, Edward Berkel, the one who helped her move?"

"Of course, the weasel. Your *buddy*."

"Yeah, I saw him at my yoga class last night and I pissed on his car."

"You did not!"

"Yeah."

His face turns red and puffy, mouth wide open, eyes crinkled. "That's the most beautiful thing I've ever heard."

"But I didn't want to. It just happened. Like, my body did it, but not me."

He pulls up a chair in front of me and slaps a meaty hand on my knee. "Dude, you've been through a lot with the separation and all. You always suspected little weasel dick wanted to move in on your woman. Jenna leaves you, you're bumping into this piece of shit. I can understand. He's lucky you didn't do worse."

Pause. "I backed into his car, too. Cracked it pretty good."

"Really?" he says, chuckling, his smile morphing to a grimace. "Dude, that's pretty serious."

I go on to tell him about the deer and the meat. "I think I need to see a psychiatrist or something."

"You could see mine, Dr. Feinman. He gives me all kinds of good shit: Lexapro, Xanax. You can call him tomorrow."

"Okay. Thanks, Gus." And I mean it. My wife couldn't stand him, but he's the kind of person that would walk through a burning house for you.

"So, we going riding or what?" he says, on to the next moment, like I didn't just tell him I'm losing my cookies. I look at his child-like eyes and see he's serious. "I only got till one, dude. Then I got to take the kids to their games."

"I can't possibly."

"Eh, I figured. Well, I got to ride. Work on the gut. I'll call you tonight with Dr. F's number and check on you," he says as he leaves.

I go to deal with the dishes when the front door flies open. "The retreat!" yells Gus, stomping back in.

"What?"

"The Return to Nature retreat. What was your totem?"

"Wolf."

He holds his palms in the air like *Get it?* I look at him, confused, my head still heavy.

"The whole point of the totem was to take on some of the animal's characteristics, right? Maybe it's working."

"You think?"

"Hell yes! Dude, you're finding your inner wolf. Mind-body connection. That shit is real. I told you."

"What was your totem?"

"Beaver."

"Beaver? All the animals on the planet and you choose beaver?"

"I'm a slob, a procrastinator. I'm trying to work harder. I wanted to choose something that would make my ass busy. A beaver," he says like I'm a dumbass for not figuring it out.

Gus and his wife had dragged me to this Return to Nature retreat at the Epsilon Institute for Holistic Studies earlier in the week. They thought it would help me deal with the despair I'd felt since Jenna left. I'd been up there once before, not exactly my thing, but the gesture meant so much to me, I went along. And I admit, I enjoyed it: being around warm people, the meditation, hikes, the sweat lodge. The final exercise was called "Finding Your Life Totem." You went out to the woods by yourself and did a sort of mediation, a prayer to an animal you wanted as your life guide.

I sat on a moss-covered stump, holding a wolf tooth in my palm given to me by the retreat director, Swami Dionini, and repeated the chant he gave me: "Wolf Mother, Wolf Father, my soul is an empty vessel that I offer to you to fill with your divine wolf nature: strength, courage, intelligence, power, ferocity." I kept whispering the words, breathing in the wind, my eyes narrow slits observing the woods: squirrels chasing one another through mounds of decaying leaves; jagged tree trunks and branches lying scattered about the forest floor; shadowy hemlock trees lurching and creaking in the wind. After a while the light began to fade and it got cold, but I kept chanting the words.

The conch sounded and I headed back toward the center. I couldn't tell if anything had happened, doubted it had. But as I emerged from the woods, I heard detailed conversations in the kitchen all the way across the field. I could smell individual ingredients from the evening meal wafting through the night air: lentils, paprika, fresh tomatoes. I figured all the healthy food and meditation must have gotten rid of the mental clutter separating me from the world and given me a heightened sense of my surroundings.

But once I got home from the retreat, the sensations became more subtle and sporadic. And nothing about the retreat could have caused this craziness in me—if anything, it made me calmer, more passive. Gus is just being dramatic or idealistic thinking what I'm going through has something to do with the retreat. It's loneliness, I think. Fear. I'm just broken since she's been gone.

I spend the next hour cleaning and sanitizing the kitchen. The bones and leftover meat go in a plastic garbage bag and then to the trash in the garage. Then I take a scalding shower, shave my face and groom my eyebrows. I put clean sheets on my bed and lie with a book, *The Third Chimpanzee*, and doze off.

I awake and the sunlight outside has faded to gray. I dress and set my alarm clock for work the next day.

With my book sitting on the passenger's seat, I drive toward the Green Planet Cafe in Irvingville to get a salad. I'm waiting at a red light, but when it turns green, the guy in front of me doesn't move, cell phone at his ear, absorbed in a conversation. I get a prickly sensation on the back of my neck and my jaw muscles start pulsing. I hit my horn and he edges forward, but is barely moving. "Go, go you fucking idiot!" I pull up to his rear, whip around him and race up the street. Without thinking, I drive past the restaurant and keep going for several blocks till I reach the yoga studio. I realize it's time for my regular class—it just started. The beige Prius, duct tape on one of the headlights, sits in front. I'll go in and take the class. I need it to calm down. I snatch my mat from the trunk and march in, flashing my card to the young receptionist. She seems startled at the sight of me. "Sir, are you okay?"

I turn back to her, gazing at her neckline and cleavage, sensing her organs underneath cloth and skin, smelling her young sex. "I don't know. I feel a little off. I hope the class will give me some relief," I say, leaning over the counter into her space.

"Yeah, good plan," she chuckles nervously.

I step into the studio and close the door quietly. The teacher and a few students look at me with alarm. The class is full, mid-session, and the only spots are in front by the giant river view window.

I join the class in Downward Facing Dog, pushing my hamstrings back and stretching my ass to the sky, despite being hindered by khakis and a button up. I notice a familiar scent in the air, Jenna, my ex. I jerk my head around and scan the studio. No Jenna and the scent gone. But Berkel is back there, intently focused on the pose.

My breath deepens and I push hard through each asana, my pants restraining my movements, but then ripping open at the crotch, freeing me to straddle and lunge more deeply than I thought possible.

On the third Sun Salutation, I breath it in again, her smell, wafting on the air of the sweaty room. I stand and follow the scent to *him*, now on his belly, pushing up into High Cobra. Her, her skin, her sexual juice mingling with his. He looks up at me with irritation and back to the teacher. I feel a pang in my bladder, pull out my penis and piss on his back and head. He leaps up, backing away. "What the fuck are you doing?" I hear yelps and screams in the background and see women rushing out the door, as I continue pissing on his mat, watching it flood onto the wooden floor.

"Call the police," I hear from the lobby.

He's watching me, all his fake serenity gone. "You're a sick bastard!"

I shake off the drops and zip myself back in. The yoga teacher is in front of me, eyes locked on mine. "Get out of here! Now!"

I sense her fury, smell her sweat, but something is odd. I remember my discovery about her from the other day and look at her slim belly. "You're pregnant," I say. Her inner lion crumbles, and she backs away and leaves. It's just me and him.

"There's piss on me, you fucking bastard! You pissed on me!" I look at his face, pointy and weasel-like, and think to snatch him by the throat, but I've already gone too far. I need to get out of here. I turn and walk toward the studio door. "You stay away from Jenna!"

His words claw at my gut. Blood surges to all my limbs, my muscles tighten, my face contorts. I turn and rush him. He's game, low in a Bruce Lee stance, and nails me with a kick to the abdomen. I hear screams and angry female voices yelling to stop.

The blow staggers me, but I snatch his ankle on the next one and drive him backward. I grab a handful of sweaty hair in my fist and smash his head into the wall, chunks of plaster falling to the floorboards, a cloud of dust encircling us. He crumples to the ground, his eyes glassy.

I snatch him by the collar and haul him across the room, his limp feet squeaking against the wood floor, and heave him head first through the bay window, but his arms are locked around my torso and leg, pulling me out with him. We spin to the cement two stories below on a waterfall of glass shards, our bodies entangled like kinky lovers.

I land, my chest on his, and a violent shock goes through my body. I'm stunned, unable to breath. The trees blowing in the wind and cars driving past are slow, surreal. I go to a knee, then stand. He lays prostrate and twisted like a neglected Barbie doll flung to the floor.

I stagger to my Buick and get in as two cop cars pull to the front of the building. I hear muffled voices from the studio: "We need an ambulance!" "Oh my God! Oh my God!" "I think he's dead."

I start the car and fly.

### 3

I'm driving. Fast. But where the hell am I going? What did I do? It wasn't me. It was like something in me, but not me. The thought was there, the most miniscule impulse, and it happened.

I think of him lying there twisted and feel sickened. I'm driving toward my house, but realize the cops will be there. I hook a U-turn and speed up Route 9, away from home, away from the studio.

I should just turn myself in. Find a cop station, say I was overwhelmed with grief over my wife, over the affair. The affair? Was it an affair? How long has this been going on? I feel the hairs on the back of my neck bristle. I think to go back and run him over.

I pass Saint Francis Hospital and hook a sudden left, tires screeching, rear end fish-tailing, cars honking at me. I pull into the parking lot. I'll check myself in. I've lost all rationale thought, all inner control. I'm not me.

I have the desire, but don't move, my hands clutching the wheel. I see men and women outside in pastel green scrubs. What can they do for me? Fill me full of dope. Ask about my childhood. Lock me up. They can't help me.

I turn around and go back to Route 9, racing north. I realize I have to get back to the Epsilon Institute. I have to find Dionini, the Return to Nature guy. Dionini, he put this in me, the wolf. He has to remove it.

◊ ◊ ◊ ◊ ◊

I pull into the gravel parking lot of the Epsilon Institute, the low gas light on my dashboard glowing red, and rush to the office. The young receptionist's serene expression morphs to fear as I approach. "I need Dionini. I need to see him."

"Dionini?"

"The Return to Nature guy. I need him, now!"

"I'm sorry, sir, I can't give out personal information. If you'd like to leave a mess—"

"Do I look like I'm here to leave a fucking message?" She's trembling, straining to stay composed. I take a breath. "Look, I had a bad effect from his retreat. I need his help."

"I'll get my supervisor." She disappears behind the counter and a few happy mellow people enter, but quickly turn around upon seeing me. I get a whiff of the outside as a gust of wind comes in. I run out and lift my head to smell the air. He's got to be in one of the bungalows up the hill.

I skirt around cabins, looking for signs, listening for the pompous voice, seeking his odor, a sour milk smell reeking from his pores mixed with the patchouli oil he wears.

I approach the first bungalow. I hear soft murmurs and smell men, but not Dionini. At the next bungalow I catch the scent of older females. I continue past several rooms, stopping at each. Then the voice arises like crisp tissue paper crinkling, formal, pontificating. I rap on the door several times.

His words cease and I hear footsteps moving toward the door. He stands before me, gazing without recognition, wisps of white hair blowing in the breeze, wrapped in a burgundy robe. "Dionini, I need your help."

"Who are you?"

I step past him into the room. A young woman sits on a little sofa, legs tucked under her hips. She gets a worried look when she sees me. "I was at your Return to Nature retreat last week and I need you to help me."

The suave demeanor returns. "Ah, yes, I remember you, my dear friend." He embraces my hand with both of his. "But I hardly recognized you. You look ill." He turns to the girl. "I'm afraid duty calls. We'll have to continue this discussion at a future date." She rises and moves to the door. "Good night, dear," he says as they hold each others' hands, facing one other.

"Oh, Swami Dionini, you've helped me so much, your wisdom."

"We've helped each other. Healing is always mutual."

She kisses one cheek, then the next. I'm doing everything possible not to shove her out the door. She turns to leave, but then spins back, looking at me. "He's wonderful. I'm sure he'll be able to help you." She smiles and disappears into the night. I feel a twitch in my belly. She's ripe, ovulating.

He shuts the door and faces me. "Now, sit my friend. Your humble servant. What can I do for you?"

I force myself to sit despite twitchy muscles begging to stand, run, leap. He leans back in a throne-like chair, skinny legs crossed, flaps of his robe hanging open, wispy gray hairs spiraling off his sparrow-like chest.

"The totem activity, it's taken over me."

"You don't say. Please, go on."

"I chose a wolf. Remember, you gave me the tooth. And I feel it deeply now, inside me. It's as if the wolf spirit has taken control of my mind, my body."

His eyes glow. "That's exactly as it's been described in the Jahunkee folklore. This is remarkable."

"No! I'm out of control. It's making me aggressive. I attacked someone tonight."

He's on his feet now. "This is quite unique. I've never known it to be this successful."

"It's not successful. It's a disaster. I need you to take it away."

"Take it away?"

"Yes, you have to remove it!" My heart is racing. I want to snatch him by his saggy throat and shake him.

"Listen…what's your name?"

"Dale."

"Dale, I understand you're upset, scared, but let's not be hasty." He steps closer to me. "Do you believe in universal blessings?"

"What?"

"Sometimes gifts come in frightening packages. And because of our conditioning, we often reject them. My shamanistic calling came as a dream, a chilling and confusing dream. I could have run from it."

"I don't give a shit!"

"Well, you should," he says, a hint of harshness in his voice. Then his eyes brighten again and an ugly smile slithers across his thin lips. "I would hate for you to turn your back on this. You've received something special, a gift."

I stand. "Make it go away."

"Listen, I have a retreat at Kripalu in two weeks. Why don't you come. You can demonstrate the power of the Return to Nature ritual. You see, more blessings are coming your way already."

I grab the collar of his robe and push him into the wall. A wave of fear crosses his face. "Dale, please, I'm only trying to help you. This isn't helping either of us."

"Take it away. I can't be like this."

Sober. Eyes meeting mine. "Dale, that's beyond my capabilities."

I release him. "What do you mean?"

"I've studied shamanism and the totem exercise is something I've read about. Like most of the healing arts, it's about the mind–body connection. Your mind believes, so your body becomes what you envisioned. I never dreamed it could actually possess a person this way." My knees buckle and I slump to the ground, my lower lip starting to quiver. "Dale, isn't there a part of you that wants this? The aggressiveness, the fury? You did choose the wolf, after all."

I grasp at the thought, but deny it—it sickens me. I see Berkel lying on the sidewalk. "No, that's a lie."

"No? I remember our conversation clearly now. You wanted to be strong, fierce. You were crushed about your wife, tired of being the victim. You wanted to be predator, not prey. Embrace it, Dale!"

His words reach into some deep truth that repulses me. The pissing, the violence, the fear I've created has made me feel powerful. I feel my belly heaving, the muscles battling the approaching sobs, the pain locked in my body from my loss, every loss, and the loss of myself—no, the loss of my image of myself. A low moan vibrates in my throat and forceful sobs are liberated. I wail and cry into the musty carpet.

I feel the heat of his body moving toward me. "Crying is healing, Dale."

He puts a smooth hand on the back of my neck and my stomach clenches. My legs explode, my hand shooting toward his throat. He's against the wall, purple-faced, eyes bulging. I feel loose skin and tendons clutched in my fist. I squeeze and feel something inside his neck pop. I try to rip the whole throat out, but it won't give.

I grip the side of his neck with both hands and stretch it taut, his body squirming beneath my grasp. I eye the white flesh and bite, clamping down with my canines, feeling them cut and gnash through rubber fibers, blood pouring into my mouth and spraying my face. I pull away and he folds to the ground, eyes still open, blood shooting out of the gash in his throat.

◊ ◊ ◊ ◊ ◊

At the Arco station I hand my credit card to a guy, fat and bearded with tattoos, looks like he'll shit his pants at the sight of me, and tell him to fill it. I smell processed food and though it's sickening, full of chemicals, it makes me ravenous. I grab two handfuls of Beef Jerky out of a jar. "These, too," I tell him, holding the packages against my body as I go back out to the car. I scarf down the Beef Jerky as I fill up the tank, the gas fumes gagging me.

I get in my car and speed north. I realize I forgot my credit card at the gas station, but don't bother to go back. I just eat the jerky, ripping large hunks off with my teeth and gulping them down.

As the night wears on, sometimes I observe my old self again, lurking in the background, and he feels horror at my actions. I think to kill myself, to swerve into an oncoming tractor-trailer. But then the thoughts get quiet again, buried underground. Mostly I just want to escape. To go away, north, to the country where it's desolate, where I won't be captured. They'll be looking for me and I've got to get far.

I'm startled by a loud buzzing sound. My phone. Gus. And I think how good it would be to speak to him, to not be alone with this. But what could I say? I murdered a man. He'd tell me turn myself in. I'd end up in jail, in a cage. And he'd probably convince me. I'd do it if he told me to.

I open the phone. "Hello? Hello? Dale, are you there? Hello? Are you okay?" His voice is trying to lure me back. But how can I turn back? I've gone too far. "Hello, Dale?" I fling the phone out the window into the blackness.

◊ ◊ ◊ ◊ ◊

I reach a vast mountain range as the sun is starting to rise. I make out faint outlines of the forest in the darkness, fog rising from the brush and seeping onto the street.

The road gets steeper and more curvy. My ears pop and I put the car in low gear, a hazy ray of sun shooting through the gaps of the tree line. I'm winding around cliffs, beat-up metal rails all that stand between my car and the edge of the mountain.

I come to a patch of gravel on the side of the road and pull in. I need to rest my eyes. The spot is big enough to hold a dozen or so cars and is littered with crushed beer cans and empty cigarette packs.

Ahead of me is endless green: mountains, forests, lakes. I feel the tension ease in my neck and jaw. I step out to the edge, a steep slant to a river below that looks like a skinny line of green paint from here.

Even torn in the crotch, my pants feel constraining, riding up my ass, crunching my balls. My shoes feel bulky and stiff. I pull them off, everything—shoes, pants, shirt—and chuck them down the ravine and watch them float and tumble in the wind, eventually getting stuck on trees, one shoe, I think, making it to the river.

I return to my car, the gravel painful under my feet. I sit inside the Buick, the leather seats gummy against my bare back. I look out over the horizon and know there's no turning back. I start the engine, put the car in drive and rest my naked foot on the gas pedal. The Buick edges forward, the rim of the cliff growing. I take hold of the door latch, push the door open and hop out, my feet skidding across the gravel as I attempt to keep my balance.

The Buick rolls to the edge. The nose slumps down as the front wheels disappear over the cliff. The car pauses, like a see saw dangling on a bar. Then the back end eases up and the black Buick hurtles over the mountainside. I rush to the edge and see it collide into a cluster of trees a hundred feet below, sending a door flying up toward me, but the body smashes through the trees, tumbling down the mountain till it crashes into the river. It's just a black speck now, spewing smoke on the edge of the winding green waterway.

To the side of the gravel lot is a rocky outcrop. I go to it and study the landscape, envisioning a path far to the side where the steepness is tempered. I step down below the plateau, and snake my way along the mountain through thorny shrubs and fallen trees, turning and winding, clinging to roots and stones. I look back, but the road is gone. There's only mountain now.

As I trudge forward, the wind carries an edible scent to my nose. Then I see it, a dark-colored rabbit in the brush, only a few feet from me, frozen. I feel its heart beating and sense it's warm flesh underneath the skin. I take a few steps toward it and dive, coming close, but snatching nothing but dirt clods. I get up and suck my scraped palm.

I continue down the mountainside, picking my way through shrubs and rocks. I smell something on the wind that makes my shoulders tense. I arrive at a flat gray boulder and the odor becomes harsh like ammonia, twisting my face to a grimace, drool pooling in the bottom of my mouth and dribbling down my chin. It's the smell of a hunter, a canine. I piss on the stone and the surrounding dirt till the scent is overpowered.

Mine. All this, mine.

**Floris Kleijne** has worked steadily towards a writing career his whole life. Not only by getting his short stories published and winning some awards, but also by unintentionally accumulating the sort of resume befitting a struggling writer: notary clerk, croissant baker, marketeer, scientist, trainer, camp counsellor, improv actor, and computer programmer. He's published fantasy, science fiction, horror, suspense, and kinda-mainstream-but-hard-to-pinpoint, and his ambition is to have fiction published in every genre but High Literature. He dedicates this story, his ninth publication, to his wife, whose arrival in his life coincided with the writing of it.

## TRICK OR TREAT

"Mom, it itches!"

"For God sake, don't scratch."

Jane pulled her son's right hand roughly away from his expertly painted face.

"You'll smear the whole design. Just leave it be, the itch will pass."

"But, mom..."

"No buts, Sander. I worked on your skull face for an hour. Let's try and keep it intact for more than a minute, 'kay?"

Sander's face was a grinning skull painted in an unhealthy shade of dull creamy white. His own dark eyes all but disappeared into the black holes Jane had drawn around them; his nose was a sharp black triangle; gaping and crooked teeth were painted over his lips. Jane had used a black dye to color his hair, though most of his head would be hidden under his cowl.

From the wide sleeves of his rough brown robe peeked fingers painted the same unpleasant white, and long yellow nails. His left hand clutched the shaft of the perfect prop Jane had found in Poppa's shed: a kid-sized scythe, too dull to be dangerous, but otherwise perfectly convincing. She had no idea why her father would own a tool like that, but it fitted perfectly with the Grim Reaper Sander wanted to be this Halloween.

Jane was proud of the costume job she'd done on her son, very proud. But even to herself, even though she'd spent hours preparing his costume and dressing him, he was spooky.

He looked like Death incarnate.

"Okay," he said, and that eleven-year-old voice coming from between the bone-white painted jaws was disconcerting. He turned from his mother and started for the door.

"Aren't you forgetting something, young man?"

Sander stopped and turned around with a suddenness that startled his mother. For just a moment, his robe had billowed around him and it seemed that he was wielding the scythe, not just holding it. Jane took an involuntary step backwards.

"What, mom?"

For a moment, Jane forgot to answer her son. Then she absently reached for the thing on the side table.

"Here, sweetie," she said.

"Ah no, mom! Come on, I'm eleven!"

His protest shook her out of it.

"Sander," she said, sitting up straighter on the couch, "You know this is the deal. You get to keep the candy that fits in here, no more. And don't push your luck, buster—you know how I feel about candy."

"Aw, mom." There was a slight whine in his voice, but he grabbed the lunch box with a brief smile. Jane had bought him the Scooby-Doo lunch box four years earlier and it was the perfect Halloween candy container, with images of the ghosts, mummies, monster spiders and villains the clumsy cartoon dog had fought in the TV series.

Sander objected to the lunch box every year; he wanted to bring his tote bag like other kids and take home all the candy he could carry. Jane was adamant though. She was determined to keep his teeth good and his body healthy.

"Now scoot!" she said, getting up from the couch and herding him to the door.

Sander reached for front door, and Jane was pleased to see he was careful enough not damage the artificial nails as he opened it.

As the door swung outward, a knob of white swung down, almost knocking Sander in the head. He knocked it out of his way with his scythe without a pause, mumbling, "We should have a real bone."

Jane came after him and stood in the doorway, watching him go. The quiet suburban street, its orderly succession of driveways and lawns lit by jack-o-lanterns and strings of unseasonable Christmas lights, was already the domain of small groups of children dressed up as their favorite scary characters. Most of them seemed to have found inspiration in the grimmer fairy tales, though more and more of the kids dressed up like Hollywood serial killers—or their victims.

"Have fun!" she called after her son. He waved without looking back.

Shaking her head, Jane adjusted the plastic bone over the door and went back inside. Closing the door and grabbing her unopened mail, she proceeded to turn off all the lights in the house. Then, with the mail and her latest reading project under her arm and a glass of Merlot in her hand, she made her way to the back yard and settled in her deck chair with a reading light.

She had better things to do than hand out candy to other people's children.

Jane picked up the novel from the table by her deck chair. The mail had proved a disappointment: only the postcard from her sister was of any interest, reminding her of her niece's upcoming fourth birthday. She had made a mental note to have a huge birthday cake delivered; she adored her niece and got to see her much too infrequently. Other than the postcard, the mail consisted of bills, credit card statements, advertising, and pizza delivery flyers.

The only envelope that had looked promising, with its overseas stamps and handwritten address, proved to be a crank letter from some European professor, carrying on in terrible English about the neuropsychological dangers of too much modern candy. The letter was entertaining, but the man was obviously mad. Jane was an expert on the subject of candy. She maintained a website on the dangers of obesitas, caries, and even ADHD. But even she knew candy was harmless in small quantities, and the letter turned into a mad rant after just a few paragraphs. The guy had probably found her online and hoped to find an ally in his deranged crusade. She would toss the letter into the fireplace with the empty envelopes when she went inside.

◊ ◊ ◊ ◊

The phone rang as the bombardment of Atlanta ceased. Jane had chosen 'Gone with the Wind' for her reading project, and was so engrossed in the book that the ringing of the phone felt like an anachronism. It took her a while to drag herself out of the prose and decide to answer. With Sander home, she usually let the machine pick up, but it could be him now. Something could be wrong. She went back inside to grab the cordless handset and went back to her deck chair as she pressed the Answer button.

"Hello?"

"Hello?" said an unfamiliar, accented male voice. He sounded older than her own 32 years, though she couldn't tell how much older. "This is Mrs. Goodwin, no?"

"This is Jane Goodwin speaking. Who's this?"

"You get my letter in time, Mrs. Goodwin, no?"

With some irritation, she sat back down and took a sip of her wine.

"Who *is* this?"

"I am Duchamps," he said, and both the accent and the name snapped into place. He was the crank letter writer, and the fancy stamps had been French.

"Right," Jane said, and moved the phone to her other hand to grab her book. "I'm hanging up now."

She took the phone away from her ear, and just as she was about to press the Disconnect button, she heard Duchamps shout:

"Sander is in danger!"

She snapped the phone back to her ear.

"That's nothing to joke about, mister!"

"It is not, Mrs. Goodwin. I am serious. You read my letter, no?"

"To be frank, Mr. Duchamps, I tried. If that's what you're calling about, good night."

"No, wait! Please, Mrs. Goodwin. Did you give Monkey Puffs to your son this week?"

Again, Jane halted in the process of hanging up on him.

"Well...yes, I did. They came in the mail, a free sample. Why?"

A distorted sigh came through the transatlantic connection.

"Mrs. Goodwin, there is something in those Monkey Puffs. A bad substance. If you have left, throw it away. And please, Mrs. Goodwin, do not allow your child on the trick and treat tonight!"

"You're crazy, aren't you? If there was anything in those Puffs, they wouldn't be allowed, now would they? And believe me, I checked. They're new, but they're approved."

"Of course they are!" Duchamps snapped. He sounded angry, but almost in tears at the same time. "Your FDA not knows what is the danger of this substance! I do the research at Sorbonne. Mrs. Goodwin, my rats, they attack and kill each other! Don't let your son..."

"I'm sure I don't see how murderous rats apply to my son," Jane interrupted. "Goodnight, Mr. Duchamps. Please don't call again."

Pressing the Disconnect button, Jane put the phone aside and got up to refill her glass in the kitchen. She turned on the light on a scene of chaos and mayhem. Splashes of red gave evidence to the quick meal of warmed-up ravioli; face-paint, brushes, bits of cloth and a bowl of grey water littered the bar; yesterday's dishes were in the sink, a reminder of last night's bedtime temper tantrum and the interminable phone call from her mother.

Jane put down her empty wine glass and set about straightening up the kitchen area. She was careful to wash out the brushes and let them dry properly; she had already closed the tubes of face paint. After she poured away the bowl of paint water, she quickly washed the dishes and for the thousandth time cursed her ex for taking the dishwasher.

She didn't remember taking out the whetstone last night, but while it was out she might as well re-sharpen her kitchen knives.

◊ ◊ ◊ ◊ ◊

Again, ringing pulled her out of her book. Incessant, annoying ringing. She grabbed the phone before realizing the sound came from further away. It was a different sound, one she hadn't heard in a while.

The doorbell.

It couldn't be Sander. He had his own key and was so proud of it that he insisted on opening the door even when with his mom. She had personally seen to it that he was wearing it under his robe. Not that he'd forget. It couldn't be any of the other kids that were out trick-or-treating. They could see the house was dark, couldn't they?

The police?

Jane sat up with a start. But when she went back in her mind to when the ringing started, she knew it had been this annoying and repetitive from the start. The police, she thought, would start out by ringing her bell like normal visitors.

Kids, then, after all. They'd give up soon enough.

But minutes later, every attempt to get back into her book had still been foiled by the maddening rhythm of those kids pressing her door bell every two seconds. Muttering half-remembered curses under her breath, Jane got up and walked back into the dark house. She wasn't wearing her shoes and moved as silently as she could. She meant to give those kids the scare of their lifetime.

When she was halfway through the living room, the ringing ceased.

Jane froze. There wasn't a sound from the door. She knew the darkness in her house prevented anyone from seeing in. The kids might have seen movement though. But she hadn't heard any scurrying feet, running sneakers, nothing. They might have stopped pressing her doorbell, but they were still out there, cowering in the dark.

Slowly and silently, she stepped towards the door. As she reached for the switch that controlled the outside light, she smiled in anticipation. She grabbed the door knob with her other hand and flicked the switch as she pulled open the door.

There was no one outside.

And the light stayed off.

One hand involuntarily crept to her chest. She breathed shallowly as she stepped outside. Glass crunched under her feet, and a muffled shriek escaped her. She jerked up her injured foot and stepped back. She looked up and saw the remains of the shattered light bulb over her door.

"Goddammit!"

Jane looked quickly around. She always made a point of using clean language around Sander and his friends, and didn't want any of the neighborhood kids to pick up her curses. But it was annoying. This was a good neighborhood, and acts of vandalism like this were rare. She decided to write a flyer about it the next day.

Jane pulled the door closed behind her and limped upstairs to dress the cuts in her foot. She would have to remember to sweep outside her door; she didn't want Sander—or any other kids, she reminded herself—to step in the glass as she had. In the harsh neon of the bathroom, she saw the cuts weren't too bad, and no glass had lodged in them. The band aids would be uncomfortable under her sole, but that couldn't be helped.

She stepped in front of the mirror, adjusted her hair, checked around her eyes for wrinkles.

Downstairs, the door clicked.

She could see her eyes widen and face pale in the mirror. Shit! She'd forgotten to lock the front door. She stood frozen, her face still inches from the mirror surface, breathing shallowly, listening for more sounds. But she heard nothing for what felt like minutes.

Then something screeched. Downstairs.

Jane took an involuntary step back. Her calves hit the toilet seat and she sat down heavily, creating a terrible racket in the silent house. The skin on her back crawled and her shoulders were locked, freezing her posture like a statue of terror.

It was a cat, she told herself, repeating it over and over. It was a cat. Only a puss in heat makes a sound like that. Or a peacock, but there weren't many of those in the neighborhood, were there? It must have been a cat.

Jane forced herself to stand up, get out of the bathroom, go down the stairs. Halfway down the steps, she could see the front door ajar. There was no movement outside or in. Trying to look in every direction at once, she descended the final steps.

When she stepped towards the front door to close it, she saw the object on the threshold.

It was a severed cat's tail.

◇ ◇ ◇ ◇ ◇

The police had been useless, of course. When she'd finally convinced the operator she wasn't joking, he said they might send over a patrol car next day. As far as he was concerned, it had probably been a Halloween prank gone bad. Yes, it was a sick thing to do. Yes, animal mutilation was a crime. But there was always enough real crime going on at Halloween. A cat's tail just didn't have much priority.

By the time she hung up, Jane was so furious she was no longer scared. Anyway, she couldn't afford to be scared; she was not letting Sander stay out a minute longer, even if it meant having to drag him home. Grabbing the broom from the downstairs closet, she gave the glass outside the door a perfunctory sweep before walking out into the road.

It was deserted.

The parked cars were still in the driveways, and the grinning faces of the jack-o-lanterns still shone their spooky orange light over the lawns. But there was no one outside. And all the houses were dark. She saw no movement, heard no sounds; no doorbells ringing, no kids gleefully shouting 'trick or treat!', no patter of small footsteps.

Jane ran down the road at random, shouting her boy's name at the top of her lungs. The houses were dark and nothing moved. And almost every door stood open.

"Sander! SANDER!"

She thought she saw movement in the Andrews place. She stopped running, took a few uncertain steps towards the front porch. Their door was open like the others.

"Susan?" she called out. "Jake?"

In the deep dark of the hallway, she saw movement again. Slow but determined movement. Light glinted off metal. Jane was suddenly sure she didn't want to see whatever was coming towards her. Stifling the scream in her throat, she turned and ran, sprinted back home. It seemed like she saw movement in every house now, slow, determined movement. Turning into her driveway, she crashed through her door and slammed it closed behind her. She double-locked the door, throwing the bolt and hooking the chain closed. With the phone clutched in her hands, she collapsed onto the couch.

With 911 in the display, she hesitated over the Dial button.

What was she going to say? What could she say that made any sense at all? The operator would laugh at her. It was Halloween, for God's sake!

But Sander was out there. He was out there and something was really, really wrong. She had felt it. He was out there in the wrongness. She knew she had to get up, get outside, look for him.

But she couldn't get herself to move.

◊ ◊ ◊ ◊ ◊

An eternity later, there was a noise outside the door. Jane held her breath. A low scuffing sound it was, a muffled knocking. She stared wide-eyed at the door, unable to look away, unable to move.

Then she heard a key in the lock and saw the knob turn, and Sander's muffled voice sounded.

"Mom? Mom!"

The next moment, Jane was at the door, pulling the bolt, unlocking the chain. She threw the door open and dropped to her knees, pulling Sander into a violent embrace. His scythe and lunch box dropped to the ground as he put his arms around her. She felt the grease paint of his skull face smear against her cheek.

"Are you alright?" she mouthed into his hair.

"Sure, mom," he said. She recognized his tone of voice—his face would be set in his trademark 'what now' expression. She tried to find the words to tell him how scared she'd been. But he was so obviously alright that nothing she could say would make any sense.

"I'm glad you're back," she said. "Did you get good treats?"

"Pretty good," he said, letting his arms drop and stepping back. She saw in his eyes that he was still hyped about the trick-or-treating; grabbing his hands, she could feel the stickiness of the treats that hadn't made it to the lunch box.

"We'll look at them later. You better go wash yourself, sweetie, or everything you touch will stick together!"

Sander snickered. Leaving his scythe and lunch box where he'd dropped them, he ran upstairs. Jane decided not to make a fuss about it this time. She turned around as she got up and called after her son.

"Sander?"

He paused at the top of the stairs.

"Yeah?"

"Did you notice anything funny or strange outside?"

"Nah," he said and went into the bathroom.

Jane shrugged and gave a brief self-deprecatory laugh. She was about to close the door when she decided to take one last look up and down the road. She stepped into the doorway and felt something drip on her ear. She looked up above the door and started screaming when she saw what hung there.

It was a human femur.

◊ ◊ ◊ ◊ ◊

I looked around my friends sitting around the campfire with a mixture of satisfaction and uneasy anticipation. It was my first scary story and these were the people whose opinion mattered most. Of course, I could trust Andy to be the first to speak, and to give a negative verdict, whatever he really thought about it.

"Lame!" Andy said. "Lame, lame, lame. Tell me, guys, did anyone not see that coming?"

Priscilla was staring at me with eyes wide open and a hand over her mouth. She had even paled a little. I could tell that she, at least, had not.

Robert got up out of his squat to put some more wood on the fire. I could tell by his smile that he'd liked the story, even if he did agree with Andy's verdict.

"It was creepy, that's for sure," Sam said. "Homicidal kids, mutilated cats...Just don't try doing a French accent next time. You sounded like a Cajun on dope."

"Eye ou-ill sink of sat," I said, and Sam cringed.

Then Joe sat up.

"Okay, first of all, you don't understand jack-shit about single mothers. Second of all, the whole mad scientist--dangerous substance plot has been done to death. Third of all, it just doesn't make any sense. Plus, where's the rest of the cat? Fourth of all—"

The surprise on his face when I shot him between the eyes was priceless.

"Any other critics?" I asked, looking around my circle of friends as I tossed my Monkey Puff wrapper into the flames.

**Neil Weston** is from the UK, with stories published at *The Eschatology Journal*, *Infective Ink*, *7 x 20*, *100 Horrors Anthology*, *Cuento Magazine*, *Trapeze Magazine*, *The Fringe Magazine* and *Scifaikuest* (due November 2012) amongst others..

---

## SETTING THE TABLE

The trinity of hungry Vampires gathered at the keyhole. Each observed the elderly man in the kitchen beyond. The house was unlocked, so they made their way in under the cover of a dark, early winter's evening.

Salacious voices puffed through the keyhole.

"Oh, how sweet."

"Tasty."

"Delicious."

The clock on the wall inside the room showed 5:45 pm.

The Vampires watched the man set the table. He set it and waited. An elderly woman arrived at 6:00 pm. She was neatly dressed, face powdered. The scent of violets curled towards the keyhole.

At 6:01 pm, the Vampires saw the couple sit at the table. At 6:02 pm, the woman's head lolled to the side, and she fell forward.

The Vampires sighed. Stepped back, opened the door, and entered.

One victim dead, one alive, meant the blood would be fresh.

They attacked. Flew in scatter formation, fangs like white darts…

Passed through the couple and crashed into the wall ahead.

"What the…"

"*Ouch…*"

"*Argh…*"

Their wails stabbed the atmosphere.

"What was that all about?"

"Strange."

"Spooky."

The clock on the wall said 5:45 pm.

A collective sigh.

The Vampires flicked out their bony hands in annoyance and exited the kitchen.

"How inconsiderate."

"How unfair."

"Typical.

"Bloody dead people."

At 6:00 pm, the old man then reset the table and awaited the return of his wife. Again.

**Thomas Canfield** occassionally indulges in bouts of reality but draws the line at politicians and lawyers. More frequently he can be found gazing at stars and endeavoring to penetrate the mysteries of dowsing wands.

---

# THAW

Light was just beginning to filter into the sky along the eastern horizon, pale harbinger of a dawn that seemed tentative and uncertain. A deep, pervasive silence filled the land. The truck bounced along the two lane blacktop, swerving to avoid the worst of the potholes. The headlights picked out the bare silhouettes of trees on either side, the leaves only just starting to come out. Brunot nursed a cup of cold coffee between his hands, stared out the windshield at the vast, primeval sweep of the forest.

"Well, if it isn't the salt, what would lure them down here?" he asked.

Hollinger, the park ranger, flicked a quick look at Brunot. He scratched the stubble beneath his jaw, steered with one hand resting on the wheel. "I'd rather you see them first, then make up your own mind. I don't want to influence your thinking. You may have a different take than me." Hollinger checked the mileage on the odometer, his expression set and grim. "At first, I thought it *was* the salt."

Salt was what attracted the moose, Brunot knew. They had to have salt in their diet. Most of the year they could acquire it from food sources in the wild. But in the spring, when the thaw set in, the best source of salt was runoff along the roadway.

"That's the obvious explanation." Brunot made a gesture with one hand, a characteristic mannerism that signified impatience. "Of course, if what you say is true, if there is some sort of unknown animal species, then maybe we'll have to throw the manual out. Maybe we'll have to come up with a whole new set of rules."

Unknown animal species! Brunot had to bite his lip to keep from laughing. The idea was so preposterous, so inherently absurd, that Brunot could not talk about it with any degree of seriousness. Even out here, in this sprawling Provincial Park that stretched for miles in every direction, it was impossible.

"I don't know that it's the rules that are bad." Hollinger shook his head. "But somebody, somewhere, dropped the ball on this one. That's certain."

Brunot did not say anything. It wasn't necessary. New animal species did not simply appear out of the blue—not in this day and age. Brunot was a biologist at McGill University in Montreal so he could speak with some authority on the subject. The Department Head had asked him to fly up here not because he attached any credence to the ranger's reports but because he wanted to find out what the hell was going on.

Brunot had developed a theory already: Hollinger had acquired a taste for alcohol. He looked like he drank. His eyes were bloodshot and he had not ventured within shouting distance of a razor for several days now. His jacket and trousers were rumpled and disheveled, as though he had slept in them. His hair spilled over his collar in an untidy mess and his nails were bitten to the quick. Not that Brunot could blame him for drinking. Working the winter up here, in the middle of nowhere, what else was there to do? Any man would be driven to drink. But Hollinger had let it go too far. He had let it get the upper hand—and that was bad.

"This stretch of road, I'm guessing this will be our best bet." Hollinger thumbed the headlights off. Dawn shed a gentle glow over the land. "I come through here, there are almost always moose about." They had driven twenty, maybe twenty-five kilometers out of town and had not seen another car. This time of year the Park was deserted. Hollinger swung into a gravel pullout that offered an unobstructed view of the road and of miles of virgin forest stretching away into the distance. He cut off the engine and silence spilled into the cab from outside.

"We didn't drive out here looking for moose, I hope?"

Hollinger threw a peculiar look at Brunot. "After a fashion we did, actually." The ranger opened the glove compartment, slid out a pair of binoculars. He set them on the seat.

"I don't follow you."

Hollinger studied Brunot a long moment, his expression not entirely free of contempt. "You asked me about the salt, remember? It's the salt that draws the moose here. But species X, I figure it's the moose that draw them."

Brunot sat up straighter in the seat, stared at Hollinger. "That's not possible," he said.

"Why isn't it?"

"Wolves and bears are the only natural predators for moose. And they prey on calves or weak and sickly specimens. No animal wants to target a healthy moose."

"That's what I thought, too. And then I started discovering the carcasses—big males in their prime stripped almost to the bone. Think that didn't make me sit up and take notice? What I'm talking about, it hasn't been documented before. Not to my knowledge."

Brunot stared off over the forest stretching north all the way as far as a man could see—dark and primeval, cloaked in mystery, wellspring of ancient fears. "Nobody said that these animals were carnivorous. That wasn't in your report."

"I must have forgot." Hollinger offered a thin smile. "That'll happen when you're isolated way up here. You start speaking in monosyllables after the first month or so. Your vocabulary becomes fixed at about fifty words. Just the basics. Things like food, sleep, beer. The next thing you know, why, you stop talking altogether. Stop talking and thinking both. It's that bad." Hollinger's eyes shone with a feverish light. "Or maybe, maybe I was hedging my bets. I didn't figure you'd come if I told you everything straight off. You wouldn't have believed me."

Brunot looked away. Perhaps he *had* been too quick to dismiss Hollinger's claims. Perhaps his tone *had* been too flip. He had not bothered to hide his skepticism or conceal his doubts. But the whole notion of a new species was so far beyond the bounds of probability that it warranted no other reaction. It flew in the face of everything Brunot knew to be true.

Hollinger handed him the binoculars. "Take a look," he said.

Brunot held the binoculars to his eyes. He focused on a spot maybe three hundred meters down the road. A moose had slipped out of the woods and was lapping at a puddle alongside the blacktop. It was a large male, over nine hundred pounds, a formidable animal that could hold its own against any predator. If there were wolves or bears about they would seek easier pickings elsewhere.

Brunot lowered the binoculars. "What now?" he asked.

"We wait."

Hollinger cranked open his window. The scent of pine filled the cab, cool and refreshing. All was quiet. The sun pushed above the horizon, thin streamers of mist rose over the treetops. A second moose appeared, closer than the first. It crossed the road, sampled the water, driven by the salt-hunger that could not be ignored. It was another male and moved with placid ease, taking its time. It didn't appear to notice the truck. Or, if it had, it didn't appear to care.

"What does it look like, this carnivore of yours?" Brunot asked.

Hollinger grunted. He ran his hand back and forth over the steering wheel. He was silent for so long that Brunot figured he did not mean to answer. "It's hard to describe," the ranger said at last, his voice hoarse. "It's maybe so big, the size of a bear. But quicker. I never seen anything move so fast. They're cat-like—puma, panther, jaguar. First time I saw one I thought that maybe..." Hollinger stared off into the distance, his eyes remote, filled with some memory that he did not wish to recollect. He wet his lips with his tongue. "Vicious: That's the impression that they convey. I was flat out scared. I'm not ashamed of saying so. The details, they kind of get swallowed up in that."

Brunot stirred in his seat. Perhaps there was something out there. Nothing so melodramatic as what Hollinger was suggesting—but *something*. Global climate change had resulted in species altering their usual habits and patterns of behavior. They might be compelled to stray further afield in search of new sources of food. If there were a thaw up north, the ancient sheets of ice receding, who was to say what the consequences might be?

The moose's head snapped up. The movement was so sudden, and so unexpected, that Brunot seemed to share its sense of alarm. The animal took three steps out onto the blacktop, the clopping of its hooves audible. It snuffled at the air, perplexed and confused. Its unease was palpable. It started to head east then reversed course and headed toward the truck.

"What is it doing?" Brunot exclaimed.

The moose froze. It simply stopped moving. It seemed transfixed; a deer caught in the glare of oncoming headlights. Something bolted out of the forest, a blur of dark fur and rippling muscle. It charged the moose, clipped its hindquarters. The moose gave a hoarse bellow of pain. Its rear flank had been ripped open. It began to run then, blindly, with no thought other than to get away. In quick succession one, two and finally a third cat struck at it, in and out with devastating quickness. The moose went down.

A furious struggle erupted in the bushes alongside the road. The moose's hooves lashed at the air. All around it the carnivores darted in and out, their dark pelts becoming dappled with blood. Five of them swarmed in a pack around the stricken moose.

Brunot gripped the dashboard. His heart hammered in his chest. He felt trapped as the moose was trapped, doomed as the moose was doomed. He flicked a glance at Hollinger who was watching the carnage with glassy eyes.

"Get us the hell out of here!" Brunot yelled.

Hollinger reached for the keys in the ignition. "Yeah, maybe I should do that." He started the engine. One of the cats looked up. Its eyes radiated pale fire.

"Sweet Jesus," Brunot declared in disbelief.

Hollinger spun the wheel, punched the accelerator. Gravel shot out from beneath the rear tires. The truck slewed back and forth, careening along the shoulder.

"What are they?" Hollinger demanded. "You've had a chance to look at them. Tell me what they are!" The ranger was peering back over his shoulder, out the rear of the cab.

Something slammed against the sheet metal. Brunot started in horror. The creatures were attacking the truck. They had abandoned the moose and were pursuing this new threat, intent upon destroying it. It made perfect sense. To them the truck was just another predator, encroaching on their territory, competing for their kill.

"God damn it!" Hollinger swung the wheel sharply and the front wheels found pavement. "Here comes another one! What in god's name are they?"

Brunot was sweated to the seat, frozen in shock. Not a new species. Nothing of the kind. But an old one, very old. There was no mistaking what he was looking at.

"Saber tooth," he said and his voice was a thin whine of protest.

"What?!!"

"They're saber tooth tigers." Brunot was clutching at the dash in front of him, hanging on for dear life. He felt sick. The melting permafrost, the crumbling glaciers that had gripped the far north since the height of the last Ice Age—this was their progeny; this was what they had let loose upon the world.

"The poor moose." Hollinger's eyes were filled with genuine pain. "It hasn't a chance." The truck began to accelerate on the asphalt. Brunot thought for a brief instant that they were going to make it, that they were going to escape unscathed. He almost drew a full breath.

One of the cats vaulted into the bed of the truck. It was a superb creature really, Brunot could not help thinking, an artfully crafted instrument of destruction. A paw smashed against the rear window, shattering the glass. Brunot recoiled before a flurry of claws inches from his face. The sleeve of Hollinger's jacket was shredded. Blood soaked through his clothing in a rich, dark tapestry. Both men stared at the wound in fascination. The truck veered across the road. Hollinger hit the brakes at the last instant but the vehicle skidded along the shoulder and over the side, slung sideways, coming to a halt with a violent shudder.

Brunot found himself wedged between the dash and the seat, aware of a vague, persistent pain in his side. He stared out through the windshield, waiting for death to claim him. When it did not appear he struggled to work himself free, squirmed into an upright position. He found Hollinger pinned between the doorframe and the steering wheel. His neck was broken. He was dead. His eyes stared sightlessly up at nothing at all. The Park Service badge stitched on his uniform was awash in blood.

Brunot rested his palm on Hollinger's forehead, as though to comfort him. He felt in some measure responsible for his death. Had he listened to what Hollinger was telling him, really listened, all this need not have happened. Now Brunot had to make it up to him. He had to get the word out.

Brunot eased out of the cab of the truck, clutching at his ribs. He climbed up the embankment onto the shoulder. There was no sign of the saber tooth. The enveloping silence was absolute, as vast, sprawling and inviolable as the uninterrupted stretch of forest.

Brunot stared off down the blacktop, calculating the odds of making it back in to town without encountering one of the cats. His one, his only chance seemed to be that the saber tooth would reckon him too poor and too mean a target to be worth pursuing. Brunot could not forget the look of the moose when it first caught the scent of the big cat—a look equal parts despair and incomprehension. Brunot had always been convinced that extinction meant forever. As a biologist he regarded it as a great tragedy. But now he was forced to reconsider.

Perhaps, with some species, extinction was the best of all possible outcomes.

**Terrie Leigh Relf** is a lifetime member of SFA, an active member of HWA, and is on staff at Sam's Dot Publishing. Her recent releases include *The Waters of Nyr, Poet's Workshop—and Beyond*, and *The Ancient One, Book II of The Blood Journey Saga*, co-authored with Henry Lewis Sanders. Upcoming releases from Sam's Dot Publishing include *The Wolves of Glastonbury*, co-authored with Edward Cox, *Origami Stars & Other Tales*, and the tentatively titled *Jupiter's Eye Redux*. Contact Terrie at tlrelf@gmail.com or visit her website (in progress) at http://www.appleseedhosting.com/tlr/.

## NEIGHBORHOOD WATCH

Thin slivers of moonlight pierced through the blinds of Patrick's bedroom. He was in a world of pain, his head and jaw on throb, neck and shoulder muscles bunched and stiff.

"Feeling any better?" his neighbor, Maxi, asked, settling fresh ice bags on either side of his jaw. He grimaced, hoping it translated as a smile. He'd only lived in the building a few months, and felt guilty at her kindness, especially given the matter of his little secret.

"There now. That should help a bit. I'll get you another pill and something to drink it down with."

Patrick nodded thanks. Why wasn't he healing, and what on earth had happened the other night? All he could remember with any clarity was Maxi crying out and rushing to his side as he stumbled down the hall, a bloody broken mess.

She'd cleaned him up, put him to bed, murmured something about neighborhood watch, that she was their building's coordinator.

"Here we are!" Maxi said brightly as she returned with a breakfast tray. His vision was still blurry, but his sense of smell was on overdrive. She raised his head, gently slipped a small pill, followed by a thin straw, past his lips.

They locked eyes as he took a tentative sip…O+, and warm.

# DENTAL SCAM

Patrick tilted his head and opened his mouth in front of the mirror. Still nothing, but at least the gaping holes had filled in.

Dr. Harlow, the dentist who had pulled them, had been sympathetic. "They'll grow back. Give it time. Not all vampires heal the same."

How much time, Patrick wondered, as it had been several weeks, and frankly, he was too embarrassed to go out. Not that he could feed if he did...He had an image in his mind of gumming the necks of unsuspecting college students. All he'd give them was a hickey.

The bloody dentist had actually suggested dentures to him. What self-respecting vampire wore dentures?! But he had ordered them and groaned, imagining a life of drinking reheated blood from a cup.

Patrick closed his mouth, returned to his bedroom and reached for his computer. There was a horror con coming to town, and his dentures should be ready just in time...

Patrick scanned the panel topics, scrolled through the usual costumers, assorted publishers, Steampunk gadgets and accessories before doing a double-take on Harlow's Vampire Emporium. Nah, couldn't be the same Harlow.

Patrick clicked on the link and was instantly barraged by image after heart-wrenching image of realistic looking vampire teeth.

He knew they were real.

**Jeni Decker** lives on a farm in rural Michigan with her husband, two autistic sons, an Australian Shepherd and an albino frog named Humbert Humbert. She is the author of *I Wish I Were Engulfed in Flames* and the co-author of *Waiting for Karl Rove*. You can find her blatantly exploiting her children (as well as politicians) on her blog: closetspacemusings.blogspot.com.

---

## eROTic

### NOTICE OF QUARANTINE

Pursuant to the section of the United States Containment act (Section 145, subsection 6667) guidelines set forth by the Center for Disease Control, and following the public hearing required under the Department of Human Services Contagion Response Team, the entire campus will be under FULL QUARANTINE until further notice. Students are advised to take all precautions recommended during a Class III Zombie Outbreak and should report to the Health Center if they begin to exhibit any symptoms. For more information check with the CDC's website. All attempts to enter or exit any quarantined area will be met with lethal force. Thank you for your cooperation. ~ Contagion Response Team

◊ ◊ ◊ ◊ ◊

My girlfriend turned into the perfect woman overnight. She's technically an animated cadaver now but I think I've got a few weeks until the situation becomes unsavory. She was bit two days ago and as luck would have it, I was there to come to her rescue. Okay, I was stalking her at the time but that doesn't seem to be a bone of contention between us any longer.

Annie wasn't exactly my girlfriend until she got infected, but I consider that a technicality. I know her favorite soap (Caress), what she has (or used to have) for breakfast every morning (Special K with strawberries), and that she used to paint her toenails every Monday night while watching *House*. I think she really dug the guy because, from my vantage point in the tree outside her dorm window—and judging from the increasing vibrator speed—it looked like she got more turned on as the star of the show became more abrasive. The fact that she picked up two more packs of triple-A batteries last week told me Hugh Laurie was doing *something* right.

For some reason, I thought zombies would be more menacing. The adjectives slow, bumbling, insipid and daft are better words to describe the group of dead idiots rambling around outside the college campus. They have trouble walking, never mind scaling the seven foot fence that was put up for our protection.

Isn't it ironic that stupid is catching? I'd always known it but now there's scientific proof. The fact that it all started in a local methamphetamine lab shouldn't surprise anyone. The social rejects who operate those places are only a few misfiring protons and electrons short of being zombies themselves.

But now they've *really* gone and done it. Our campus is just a skid mark off the dirty pair of skivvies that is the nearest I-95 off ramp, so I'm pretty sure it's already spread like scabies in a titty bar.

Truckers + meth addicted zombie hookers = Global Outbreak.

On the day it happened, Annie had spent the better part of the morning watching Trevor Lang repeatedly bump into the hedge circling the campus, scratch his head and then do it all over again. Poor Trev. He barely blinked when his scrotum dropped to the lawn as he masturbated into a shrub. When he bent over and popped his ball sack into his mouth, Annie stepped away from her dorm window and closed the curtains. I guess she'd held out hope for her ex-boyfriend... until he ate his own nuts.

She's not the same girl anymore. Now she's the perfect girlfriend. *My* girlfriend. She can't talk but she moans a lot. That, my friends, is a turn on. She's kind of dull so I get to provide the clever bon mots in our relationship.

Okay, so she's starting to smell. Big deal. I had a small stockpile of strawberry scented lube and I've slathered her with it. So far the smell is manageable—and further on the upside, I don't have to shower every day. It's a win-win situation as far as I can see.

The act of love is blissfully meaningless to her so it's all about my gratification. And get this—zombies are single-minded and wholly focused on one goal: food. All I had to do was teach her to eat while servicing Professor Peckerwood at the same time. It was actually pretty simple.

Breaking into the local morgue to secure human remains wasn't the most fun I've had on a Saturday evening, but it was easier than I expected. Now I have a cooler with a smorgasbord of human body parts on ice.

Then, inspiration hit one night at 3 a.m. while I watched TV.

Enter the Shake Weight. You've seen it, right? A bit of tutelage with the upper-body exercise tool in question and as soon as I introduced some yummy treats to the mix, Annie was more than amenable to multitasking. One hand for me, one hand for her. She's got a voracious appetite; Mama gets a frozen heart, Daddy gets an energetic hand job. I very well may have stumbled upon the relationship of a lifetime.

I can personally attest to the validity of the claims listed on the Shake Weight website:

- Shake Weight Utilizes New Workout Technology Called *Dynamic Inertia*, which can increase Muscle Activity to nearly 300% compared to a Standard Dumbbell.*

(My gal may be dead, but she's got some seriously awesome guns.)

- Get Incredible Results in Just 6 Minutes a Day

(I get incredible results six times a day for around six minutes at a time, though I'm usually too dizzy afterward to check the clock.)

- Designed Specifically For Women

(It may have been designed specifically for women, but if this catches on—and it will once I upload some video to my YouTube account—I think the inventors can safely change that last product claim to: Designed Specifically For Women To Benefit Men.)

Since Annie hasn't figured out how to unlock the door, she's at my beck and call. All I have to do is re-direct her frustration at not knowing where she is and what she's supposed to be doing. This morning she spent two hours trying to get a human hand out of my footlocker using a Rubiks cube. She's so *cute* when she's irritated.

"Nothing could be finer than a dip in your vagina every *moooooornin'*." I jumped up onto the bed. Annie sat with her back against the headboard, glaring at me and jerking the Shake Weight up and down with increasing speed.

I turned around and gave her a view of my backside. "Check out this keister, honey. Cuteus Maximus, right? Am I right?"

Annie groaned and jerked the exercise tool faster, causing her tits to jiggle frantically.

"How about a nice liver and brain frappe?" I opened the cooler, pulling out the ingredients and popping them into my blender with a handful of ice. I learned pretty quickly that liquefying dinner made sex more palatable. While watching her gnaw on a bloody roll of human intestine the first time she jerked me to orgasm had been a novelty, it isn't something I'm interested in repeating.

"Mwaaaaaauggggggaaaaa," Annie groaned. Blood bubbled from her mouth.

"Now, now. Patience is a virtue." I popped a straw into the cup of iced remains and held it just out of her reach while using my other hand to motion for her to spread 'em.

Annie tossed the exercise tool across the room and glowered at me with dead eyes. Somewhere along the line, my prim puss had turned into a cantankerous cunt.

"Don't be that way, darlin'." I rolled on top of her, handed Annie her dinner and slowly started sucking her left nipple. Annie latched onto the straw like a piggy at a teat. I took her groaning as evidence of my tit-ular prowess, sucking harder until her nipple came off in my mouth. I know beggars can't be choosers, but it's a tad disconcerting to have a nipple in your mouth when it's not attached to a boob.

I swear I saw a slight glimmer of satisfaction in Annie's eyes.

I spit the nipple onto Annie's stomach, rifled through my bedside drawer and pulled out a tube of Super Glue, which has become a staple of our physical relationship. After correcting the offense to her areola, I tossed the tube back into the drawer and sat at my computer, pulling up the music clip I worked on last night. I quickly adjusted the webcam, hit record and jumped up on the bed. The lyrics were inspired, sung to the tune of Queen's *Bohemian Rhapsody*. I'm going to get billions of hits!

Behind me, Annie slurped away as the musical intro blared from the speakers of my iPod docking station. I grabbed a banana to use as a microphone, singing into it:

"Is this my real life?
Can it be so easy?
Need formaldehyde
Is this my stark reality?
Look at her eyes
Gunked up with sticky debris
She's just a poor girl (poor girl), who's now a dead body
Sometimes that's the way things go
How it started, I don't know
Everyone who gets bit, infection turns them to zombies..
zombies..."

I pumped my pelvis, Professor Peckerwood slap-slapping my stomach and thigh in time with the music.

"Drama! A dead woman
Like a big, stuck pig she bled
Looks much better with her head
Oh yeah, sewed it right back on

Now it's time for both of us to play
Karma! Ooo-ooh
Would you rather that I lie?
I'd like to say we won't have sex tomorrow
(but) she's so blonde, she's so blonde, even where it matters…"

I clenched and unclenched my ass for the camera while batting Annie's face with my woody.

"My temptress, tight as a drum
*Sans* clothes she's so divine.
I don't think that it's a crime!
Annie, my cadaver—think you should know
Gotta bathe before our stink becomes uncouth
Drama!, ooo—(anyone who dies knows)
I don't want to lie
I sometimes wish I didn't find death enthralling…"

I strummed my fake air guitar during the short guitar solo and when the tempo picked up, I straddled my beautiful cadaver, sliding inside her easily due to the aforementioned strawberry lubricant.

"I do a little pirouette, I mount Annie
Scaramouche, Scaramouche, pumping horizontal tango
I've been hit by lightning—every sense is heightened…me
Galileo, Hot Potato, ripe Tomato, hold the Mayo,
Galileo quid pro quo—simpatico-o-o-o…"

Finished with her human frappé, Annie tossed the empty cup across the room, eyeing me with newfound interest. Continuing to sing, I jumped off her, disengaging painfully. I pulled the lid from the cooler and fetched my love a handful of intestines.

"I'm a geeky undergrad, nobody loves me

She's just a dead girl, who will tell her family?
Spare me your hatred for my atrocities
Easy if I go slow—no one has to know
It's a PALL! No—no one will ever know—let her go
It's a PALL! no one will ever know—let her go
It's a PALL! no one will ever know—let her go
Can not let her go—let her go (never)
Never let her go—let her go
Never let her go—ooo
No, no, no, no, no, no, no—
Oh mama mia, diarrhea, North Korea let her go!
Now here's the rub—I know there's something wrong inside
of me…of me…of me…"

As Annie slurped down intestines behind me, I approached the camera and addressed my future Youtube audience.

"Do you think I'm the ointment, or am I the fly?
Do you think somewhere inside I've already died?"

I swiveled back around and sang to Annie. She licked the blood from her fingers and burped.

"Oh Annie—can't do this to me, Annie
I gotta find out, just wanna take you from the rear…"

I tossed my faux microphone to the floor and leaped onto the bed, grabbing Annie and rolling her to her stomach as I entered her, doggy style, while whispering the final verse into her ear.

"Ooh yeah, ooh yeah
You've got no grey matter
Even I can see…
You've got no grey matter, but it doesn't matter, to me…"

**Jeff Hemenway** writes from his home in Sacramento, California. He enjoys singing with the radio and likes to believe he's pretty good at it. He likes to believe a lot of things that are demonstrably false, which is probably why he started writing fiction in the first place.

---

# GRAY

In hindsight, Franco supposed he should have never listened to the Gray Man.

But insomnia gets inside you. It grows within, like a cancer. Pretty soon it's all that's left. Reality becomes molten. Boundaries break down, everything bleeds together until life is nothing but a jumble of indistinguishable nuances.

When sleep fails long enough, it's impossible to be certain of anything.

In hindsight, Franco supposed he should have better listened to the Gray Man.

It was Saul who first pulled him into urban exploration. Saul had always ridden the line between casual thrill-seeker and balls-out danger junkie, ever since he and Franco were kids. He was the first to get into coaster parks. He was bungie-jumping before most people even knew what bungie-jumping was. He wasn't in for base-jumping or cliff-diving, none of the crazy-stupid bullshit that got you killed as often as not. He was just into the sleek, black rush of the thrill.

Franco had been working the teller window at the Seattle First National when Saul came in and asked him out to lunch. Saul had that look, that jittery energy he always possessed when he'd discovered something New and Exciting, like he'd been freebasing caffeine. Franco knew that look. Last time it had been spelunking. A good portion of Franco's right shin had been surrendered in a cave somewhere in Eastern Washington, probably chewed up by a fat, blind cave rat and hurked back up to feed its litter. If that was something rats did; Franco didn't know.

But Saul would.

Saul was a person who would know whether or not cave rats offered half-digested gunk to their squealing litter, and once you understood that, you understood half of everything there was to know about Saul.

The other half was this: Saul was the sort who would really be into something like urban exploration.

"Urban exploration," repeated Franco.

"Yeah," spat Saul through a mouthful of fried chicken tenders. For Saul, there was only one food group, and that group was "deep fried". He looked at vegetables like he expected someone to leap out and drive one through his heart. He was lithe and sinewy and had a porcelain complexion and would probably drop dead of a coronary at forty-five.

Franco sipped at his iced tea. "Exploring...urban. Stuff."

"Yeah." Saul swallowed. "It's like spelunking a little, except you're not in caves, you're in old buildings and stuff."

"Oh, that's a perfect sales point, right there. Just like spelunking. Because spelunking and I just got on like that." Franco crossed his fingers and shook them at Saul by way of emphasis.

"Well, okay, it's not dangerous like spelunking. There's no climbing into big holes, no fancy gear, no bats or whatever. It's safe, I mean. But it's...it's safe, but it sounds *wicked.*"

"Wicked. Hmm. Yeah. So we run around in deserted buildings and fend off bums. And instead of bats we get raccoons. Definitely sounds capital-W-wicked."

"Okay, man, remember after that cave you said you weren't ever listening to me again about my crazy shit, and then I promised you that next time it would be something you'd like, something safer, and you said—"

"Saul—"

"You *said* that if I found you something I could guarantee you'd like, you'd come with me. You'd give me one more shot."

"I could've fallen down and died. I could've been eaten by a cave bear."

"There weren't fucking *cave bears*, Franco. The worst thing in there was the bats. Little *pussy* bats."

"Urban exploration. And it's safe?"

"Oh, totally safe. I've looked into it. And the best part? The best part is that we live in Seattle. You know the Seattle Underground."

"Yeah, I know it."

In the late 1800s, there'd been a huge fire in Seattle. A big chunk of the place had burned to the ground, and rather than cart away the rubble and start over again, Seattle governance had decided to just build on top of the ruins. There were whole neighborhoods buried ten, twenty feet beneath the steel bustle of modern Seattle. They had a moderately renowned tour that took you underground, down fragments of road with subterranean storefronts, grime-painted remains of houses, century-old plumbing and masonry buried and forgotten. Franco had done the tour when he was nine, and he could never shake the feeling that the buildings and streets and pipes weren't all that had been sealed down below. He could imagine the rotting bones of the Old City's luckless hidden behind faded walls of once-red brick and mortar, heat-baked and brittle, gnawed thin by whatever lurked down below. And if the dead had been sealed away, then maybe a few of the living had been, as well.

"The tour's nothing, from what I've been reading," said Saul. "The tour is the pussy version. I've read about some other entrances that take you to places you wouldn't believe, only it's a little harder to get there, so the tour doesn't bother with it."

"And this is legal, of course," deadpanned Franco.

"More or less," shrugged Saul. "It's probably trespassing in a few cases, but nobody gives a crap. Nobody patrols this stuff, they just call it illegal in case some stupid kid goes in there unprepared and wanders into some old refrigerator or whatever the hell."

"Unprepared? What do we need to prepare for?"

"Nothing, nothing. Just lights and stuff. Trust me, this'll be awesome. We'll get to look at people's lives, just stopped all of a sudden and abandoned. There's stories down there. You like stories. It'll be like Pompeii. Like a slice of life from a hundred years ago."

Franco liked stories. He'd majored in anthropology in college, but life and a steady paycheck had conspired to make him a banker. He still read his National Geographics, still pored over some anthro blogs on the web. The hook was sunk deep, and now Saul just needed to reel him in.

"Maybe you could even start your own blog…" began Saul.

"Yeah, yeah, fine. I'll do it. If I get mauled by a homeless guy, though, so help me I'm never doing anything with you again."

"It'll be cool," said Saul, and crammed another lump of glistening chicken into his face. "I'll bring a can of Bum-Off."

Even if pressed, Franco couldn't have said whether the insomnia or the Underground came first. It was a chicken-or-the-egg thing, a case of positive force feedback. They grew, they expanded until they were his world, and cram banking, and cram Ally, the nice girl with the nice personality and the nice figure, and cram all of it. Franco's life became the laser-point intersection of lying sleepless in bed night after night, and crawling through the pitch-black detritus of a lost and secret world, and maybe when it came down to it those two things weren't so different.

It was cold and raining the night that Franco lost the ability to sleep. The day had slipped effortlessly from steely afternoon gray into thick nighttime gray. Ally lay next to him, naked and curled into a careless twist of flesh, blue-gray in the darkness. Her post-coital smile had faded into the bass-mouthed gawp he liked to tease her about. Air pulled in and out of her nostrils like a cheap whistle.

Franco usually slept on his side, but he drifted off on his back.

Arms flat against his torso, covers pulled up over his chest, head back, eyes closed. He'd process the previous day, putting each memory into the appropriate slot, and soon the pull of sleep dragged him below.

It was 12:47 when it first occurred to Franco that he was still awake. He'd been laying there over an hour. He wasn't not tired—point of fact, Ally had pretty well exhausted him a couple hours ago—he just wasn't *asleep*.

The rain fell outside his apartment bedroom window, patter patter against the fire-escape, against the pane. Soft and unhurried. A million tiny beats against a million tiny drums, pat-pat-rat-a-tat, and on it went, and on, and now it was 1:32.

Now it was 1:34.

Now it was 1:37.

Ally rolled over in her sleep, and now he could see the spill of her back, sleek and bare in the dark, like a ski-slope at midnight except for the lifts no lifts here no lifts but there goes one tiny skier down Mount Shoulder Blade *watch out for that mole OH NO CRASH TUMBLE NOOOOO.*

And now it was 1:58.

Had he slept yet? Had he dreamt?

The rain had stopped. All was quiet now except for the languished drone of cars three stories below, except for the little drip-drip-drip of water finding its way from roof to landing. Drip drip, fizz fizz, oh what a relief it is, and where had *that* come from, begone, pop-culture flotsam from a lost era, *I banish thee.*

And so it went, and so it went, and as the digital clock blinked its way to 5:13, Franco at last found sleep.

At 6:00, the alarm went off. He rose. He readied for work. He kissed his girlfriend goodbye and asked if she was busy tonight and reminded her to lock up before she left as if she didn't know this, and then he drove to work.

The old factory rose from the earth and pressed against the

overcast sky like a forgotten titan, curiously large against the rest of the discarded neighborhood. This was old Seattle, this was one of those little industrial chunks of city that get forgotten when a recession rolls around. The investors pull out, the squatters move in, and pretty soon it's the tragedy of the commons, writ large in graffiti and raccoon shit.

This was a modern-day ghost town.

"Jesus," said Franco, "screw the Underground, we could wander these yards for *weeks*. There's gotta be tons of stuff here, abandoned offices, factory floors, those tenements over there..." He pointed past a squat triad of office buildings, where five stories of crumbling, red architecture hinted at past residence. "This place is amazing."

"Told you, man. Urban Exploration. And this is nothing, this is the same crap they've got all over the country. This is just the surface. I Googled some pics of what sort of stuff they have down there, and man, it's wicked."

"Wicked, is it?"

Saul stretched his face in that caffeinated smile. "Capital-W, Franco."

They started walking. Each man sported an identical backpack, fresh and new from Chuck's Sporting Goods down the street from the bank, $19.95 plus tax. Saul had footed the bill. Where he got his money was anyone's guess. He was always unemployed when time came to split the lunch tab, but when it came to his obsessions he always came through.

"So," said Franco, "the entrance is in this factory somewhere?"

"Yeah. This building used to go down another level. After the fire, they built up around it and just sealed off the lower part. After it was abandoned twenty-whatever years ago, someone punched a hole in the wall and found a way down."

"Someone?"

"Yeah, guys like us, I guess, but the real pioneers. The guys who started exploration up here. They were just dicking around, I guess, and they found a place it looked like they should be able to get behind.

Grabbed a sledge-hammer, and bam. They cut a way right into the real Underground, not that sanitized bullshit you get on the tour."

"The Real Underground," laughed Franco. "It sounds so edgy."

"Well, we'll see in just a few. There's a door around that way, it should be through there and towards the back of the building."

Franco and Saul crawled over a ruined length of chainlink fence and entered the field of deceased manufacturing equipment that surrounded the building. Great fingers of rusted metal scrabbled at the sky, long-dead hulks of machinery dragged here and then forgotten.

"What the hell did this place make?" asked Franco.

"Things. Real big things."

"Thanks, Saul. You are a font of knowledge."

"Naw, usually I'd know, but you know how many places I researched trying to make this happen? It was a lot. A big number."

They walked to the side of the factory, where the rust-brown corrugated wall was broken thirty feet up by several long slits of window, and on the bottom by one smallish garage door, rolled part-way up and braced by a couple of rotted wooden slats. The windows were all either missing their glass or opaque with filth.

Saul pointed wordlessly at the open door, and they entered in a kind of quiet reverence. This was a sort of shrine, a monument to an era past. That it was also the entrance to an abandoned world seemed fitting.

Inside hung a gray mottle of various glooms. Saul and Franco each reached into their packs and drew out industrial-strength flashlights, long and blue and heavy enough to cave a man's skull. They clicked them on almost in unison and washed light over the rusted guts of a twenty-years-dead industrial wonderland.

The place had been abandoned before the robot revolution. Everything was great and heavy and looked to require a fleet of workers to keep running. Conveyor belts fed into gaping black mouths, gears brandished teeth as big as fists, great boxes of iron sprouted pipes that ran together in Gordian knots high above the floor.

If a child was asked to draw a nameless factory with unstated purpose, this would be the result.

The pair stood in an empty space just inside the door, big enough to accommodate a good-sized truck. A pile of wooden palettes rotted in one corner.

"C'mon, it's back this way," said Saul. "Good thing we brought the lights, huh?"

Flashlights, sweaters, water bottles and a box of trail mix. That was what they carried in their bags, and it seemed pathetic, now. They needed serious tools for this, they needed shovels, picks. They needed a backhoe. They needed daylight.

A great plane of stained sheet-rock formed the back wall, punctured near one corner by a makeshift doorway almost tall enough to step through without slouching. Beyond, a passageway ran between the sheet-rock and the steel exterior wall. Saul ducked his head inside and waggled his light up and down.

"Goes about ten feet, and then there's a stairway going down. Narrow. Maybe time to bust out the big guns." He reached into his pack and pulled out an industrial light wrapped in a little cage. Next came a pair of short rods, which he screwed together, and then twisted onto the end of the light. "Voila," he said, "instant torch."

"Oh shit, I didn't know you were bringing something like that."

"Always go prepared, right?" Saul smiled his grin and Franco returned it. This might actually be fun.

The stairway led down maybe ten feet, then opened into a passage sandwiched by an ancient brick wall on one side and a mound of dirt and rock on the other. Saul took the lead.

"This must be the original wall of this building, back before they rebuilt," said Franco, tapping the brick with one foot. "The corrugated metal must've come later."

Saul made a motion with his head that might've been a nod. Not far from the base of the stair, he pulled a little, white cylinder from his pack and bent it with a sharp crack. It bloomed into a brilliant green, and he dropped it at his feet.

"What's that all about?" asked Franco.

"Glow sticks," he said. "Like the ones kids use at Halloween, but heavy-duty. They last a little over four hours. These are our bread crumbs. They help us find our way back when we're ready to head out."

"You've thought of everything." Franco smiled.

"Hope so," grinned Saul, and moved on ahead. He walked slowly, holding his torch as high as the ceiling would allow, which wasn't high at all. There was room enough to walk upright, but only just.

After a couple dozen feet, the dirt wall receded enough to show off the abutting wall of brick that defined the front corner of the factory. The passage they were in jogged left. Laying on the ground against the brick, half-buried, was a square of rusted metal.

"Huh, wait up a minute, Saul." Franco knelt and picked it up. It was heavier than it looked, as if it had accumulated the weight of decades long past. "This is part of an old shovel. Look, the shaft must've come out of this hole here. Probably rotted away now, or maybe it broke off and they just tossed this aside." He turned it over in his hands. "There's something etched in it. Probably a brand name. Man, this is...this is so cool. I'm shocked it's still here, if people have been heading down here all these years..."

"It's part of the code," said Saul. "There's a code."

"There's a code?"

"Yeah. Like a...an urban explorer's code. You don't take things, you don't disturb things. Leave them for the next guys to find. We don't get to take anything with us, right?"

"Gotcha." He set the ancient shovel blade back down and stood upright. "Let's go."

"Yeah, this is nothing. I want to get into the real meat of this place. See what else is down here." Saul dropped another glowstick and they followed the passage leftward and onward.

The walkway ran a dozen yards ahead, then ended in what must have been a cave-in. A wide doorway divided the brick wall in two on their right, leading into darkness.

"This is probably right below the garage door back on the main level," said Saul. "Where we came in."

"I think this *is* the main level. At least it was. Once upon a time."

Through the door another passage ran left to right, alongside the factory's brick foundation. Rotten wood flooring defined a sort of sidewalk that fell off a few feet out into an ancient cobblestone street before being swallowed by another wall of dirt.

Saul dropped a flare.

"Left or right, buddy?"

"Eh, let's go right. I think that should lead us towards the tenements we saw topside. That could be cool."

"Right it is."

They walked largely in silence. Above them, wooden slats held up great planks of concrete. The pathway they were on jogged left and right, occasionally splitting at what used to be street intersections, where Saul would drop another flare. Often, they would have to scramble over piles of rock, or wedge through narrow slits of passage. Sometimes they had to scrape by on their stomachs through crawlspaces so narrow they had to remove their backpacks, dragging them behind with their feet.

Most of the building faces they saw were commercial, sporting walls of pitted brick or stone. A few of them still had signs of age-blackened wood affixed to the walls or lying on the sidewalk, etched with names like "Paint Store" or maybe just "Ralphs". All of them were sealed shut with planks or earth.

Franco insisted they stop every few minutes to look at some bit of historical detritus, a rusted tool, an old wagon wheel, a curious bit of masonry. Saul, for his part, was more intent on heading deeper, as if there was an ultimate discovery lying just ahead.

After what seemed like miles, Franco stopped dead.

"Oh, hey. Hey!"

"What, Franco? Did you find another bitchin' cobblestone?"

"Hey, this was your idea. No, I think this is that apartment building we saw. Look, there's no sign or anything, but this definitely looks residential. See the brick work? The other buildings were all utilitarian, but this one is just…pretty."

"Pretty? Seriously?"

"Well, decorative. You know what I mean. And the door's not sealed."

Twin rectangles of wood stood upright against the building's tremendous age. They were pale and worn, but a few flakes of blue paint still clung to the doors in odd patches. Windows bereft of glass trailed off on each side.

One of the doors angled slightly inwards.

Franco pushed it with one finger, and it swung in with a creak that shot through the Underground.

"Hey," he said, "shine your torch in there."

"We need to get going pretty soon. It's been two hours since we started, and I want to make damn sure we get back in time. I don't feel like finding our way back without the flares, you know?"

"Yeah, I just want to look inside. We won't even go in yet, I just want to peek."

Saul pushed the door in as far as it would go, and angled his torch through the opening past Franco, revealing a wide foyer. Shattered tile covered the floor. The remnants of a metal stair railing lay in pile of rubble like a giant's ribcage. Beyond it, a square of black swallowed whatever few rays of light dared approach.

"There's a doorway back there. It might go into some people's rooms or something. We've got to come back here. With more flares."

"Yeah, okay," said Saul. "Can we go now? While we still have the light from the ones we already used?"

"Yeah, that's—hey. Did you…what was that?"

"What?"

"There was…I don't know, something moved back there.

Something kind of…light colored? It was pretty big."

"Yeah, sure, it was probably a cave bear. Let's go."

"No, Saul, I'm serious. It was like this…just a flash, like someone was standing there and then he wasn't."

"The light's wiggling around, Franco. Shadows all over the damned place. Stay if you want, I'm leaving. We'll come back next weekend, try to find this place, and go inside."

They worked their way back towards the surface, back towards daylight. Backtracking was easy with Saul's flare-trail, and within half an hour they were standing in the faint drizzle of another Seattle afternoon.

"You should really come with us next time," said Franco. The lights were dim here. A name was scribbled on the paper tablecloth, something that might have been "Terry." The waitress hadn't yet mastered upside-down writing. His veal parmesan was lukewarm.

"Do I really look like the cave-diving sort," said Allie through a smile.

"They're not caves, I told you. They're…I don't know, remnants. Little bits of city that got buried. It's pretty great."

"So, what did you find that's so great?"

"I found, umm. A shovel."

"A shovel."

"Well, most of a shovel. The blade."

"So, half of a shovel. Sounds keen."

"No, really…Maybe it's an anthro thing, but it's just so cool seeing what the city was like back in the 1800s. Back before the fire ate everything, you know?"

"No, no, I'm serious. Maybe next time you'll find the other half of the shovel."

Franco smiled in resignation. "Okay, it's probably not for everyone. But honestly, it was really great. I figured it would be…about on par with Saul's other daredevil stunts, but I can't wait to go back down there."

His teeth grated against damp gristle.

"Next time, I get to choose where we eat."

"Veal's not any good?" she asked.

"Bland." He reached for the salt.

"Sorry."

"Eh, no worries."

They ate in silence. Allie's hair was pulled back in a ponytail. Bare, white shoulders stark against the black satin of her blouse. She looked great tonight, but thoughts of her, of this dinner, were slight. Tickles against the stone slab of his exhaustion. Franco tried to count the days since his last night of sleep and failed. One, two, many. Numbers lost their meaning.

"So, you're going again, then?" asked Allie.

"Yep. Saturday."

Franco chewed.

Later he lay in bed, hands laced behind his skull. Allie slept; he didn't. The clock ticked away discrete bits of night and Franco lay there, not sleeping.

Shadows danced in slow motion across his room as clouds outside paraded past the moon. The clock ticked. Allie turned over. She muttered, she snored, she muttered. She turned over again.

And Franco lay there, not sleeping.

Ancient gray cobblestones flitted through his mind, a rusted shovel blade, twisty little corridors snaking beneath the city as it bustled as it hustled as it hurried through its day very awake very much awake so very awake. Wooden planks smooth and shiny with age with wear, building facades hinting at past function, signs etched painted carved with markings that might have been language, streets long-dead, a flash of bright gray just at the edge of vision.

If Franco had slept, he would have dreamed of that peripheral fuzz, that vague promise of something, but he didn't sleep. There were no dreams, only thoughts, and soon all the thoughts were gray.

It rained on the day Franco first met the Gray Man. Not a hard rain, just a pattering afterthought, as if the clouds had let their attention drift and loosed a few stray drops. The discarded metal beasts littered across the factory yard glistened wetly and the ground was not quite muddy. There were almost puddles. Franco almost wished he'd brought an umbrella. He could almost forget that he hadn't slept in over a week.

Saul had brought more flares this time, just in case. They made their way beneath the ground, weaving amongst the twisty corridors, around piles of dirt and debris. Saul had an impeccable direction sense that Franco envied, and they found their way back to the buried apartment building in just over thirty minutes.

Franco took the lead, and the torch, as they stepped through the double doors and into the building's foyer.

"This place looks more upscale than I would've thought," said Franco. "The places above are real slums, but this looks like it was almost, almost posh."

"Posh," echoed Saul. "Yeah, this is some real grade-A dirt."

"No, I mean…look at this tile." He poked at a dust-covered shard with his toe. "This is marble. And that banister over there is brass, I'm pretty sure. Most places back then would've had wood floors, wood banisters. Cheap paint, but look, I think this place had wallpaper." He aimed the electric torch at one wall. Fingers of paper hung in curly-cues. Holes punched in the sheetrock bared the building's wooden skeleton beneath.

"So, what's through there, you think?" asked Saul, pointing at the black maw behind the twist of ruined banister. "Hallway down to some of the apartments?"

"Yeah, that'd be my guess. Wanna go check it out?"

"Oh, hell yeah."

Franco led again.

It started as a hallway. The marble flooring had given way to bare dirt; Franco wondered audibly what might have covered them once upon a time, before the fire, before the Underground was buried and sealed off. The walls held most of their sheetrock, mottled brown-gray and crumbling with age. If there had been wallpaper here it had long since rotted away. Doors to the left and right hinted at living quarters beyond, but they were invariably blocked by debris. Sometimes there were no doors left at all, and the pair had to clamber over mounds of dirt that grew in the hall like tumors.

Seventy feet and two rightward-bends later, the passage dead-ended into a door. Franco gave it a perfunctory push and almost stumbled as it unexpectedly swung inward a few inches.

"Oh shit, it's actually functional," he said.

"Hey, lucky us. Push it open, see what's in there."

With some strong urging, the door scraped inward just enough to allow passage. Behind, a stairway dipped into darkness like black paint.

Saul dropped another glowstick and Franco nodded, then the two trod gingerly down the steps. Several were missing and several more had rotted into black honeycomb, but the stair was short. They had dropped maybe ten vertical feet when they hit the floor.

At the base, a short tube of stone ran into a wall of large, gray cinderblocks and angled rightward. They stepped forward slowly, the better to let sleep the secrets that lay here, twenty feet or more below the sun.

Saul squeezed past Franco and crept down until he reached the bend.

"It goes on a bit, and it looks like there's a little room at the end. Maybe maintenance, or something?" He waggled his flashlight down the corridor.

Franco walked forward as Saul continued towards the corridor's terminus, but stopped at the cinderblock wall.

"Hey, it's all chipped away here." He poked at it with one finger. The blocks were brittle. A chunk of rock the size of a fist tumbled down from the wall and shattered against the ground, an explosion in the dead quiet of the apartment building's sunken gut. A tiny hole perforated the wall where the chunk of rock had been, staring outward like a sightless black eye.

"There's a space back here," said Franco. If Saul heard him, he didn't show it.

Franco shined his light through the hole; it illuminated nothing. The wall might have been the edge of the universe.

"What's back there?" he muttered, then cried out and jumped back.

"What? What?" shouted Saul, running over. "You okay?"

"Yeah, yeah, fine." Franco shined his flash at the wall, but from a distance this time. Nothing, no motion, just that sucking blackness. "Fine. Jumpy, I guess. My nerves are shot. Haven't been sleeping well."

"Oh. Well, try not to give me a heart attack next time your nerves jump out and yell 'Boo', right? Hey, come over here, there's this storage room, bunch of old tools, and there's a box in there on the floor. Might be something good inside."

Franco didn't mention that what he thought he saw beyond the cinderblock wall was a slender, gray face. He did not mention the cavernous eye sockets or the bright, gray irises. Gray skin, smooth like alabaster. Thatch of charcoal hair. He did not mention that the face had been trying to speak.

Inside the box was a pile of old rags. They crumbled at the touch.

...lying in bed lying awake Allie muttering softly in her sleep...

...2:33 says the clock 2:36 says the clock time to sleep says the clock time to rest time to sleep...

Eyes open and it's too bright in here even with the lights off blinds closed no moon and the jagged rattle of rain above.

Eyes closed and still it's too bright too loud too much and Allie snuffling beside him snoring beside him quiet be quiet *why can't you be quiet* and he kicks at her and again.

*Nguh what was that for* she says and he answers *You're too loud, you're snoring, I can't sleep.*

She rolls over and it's quiet but soon it's 2:51 it's 2:59 it's 2:64 and the sounds again the snoring the talking and he kicks again.

*Ow, what the hell* she says *you're still snoring* he says *I can't sleep with your goddamn snoring* he says.

*Well, you don't have to kick me so damned hard. You want me to go home, or something?*

*Yes* he says *could you* he says and time passes and now he's alone in his bed, but still it's too loud the rain the cars even the air is noisy and the blankness behind his eyelids is a nuclear glow and now it's 3:72 and now it's 3:141 and there will never be sleep again never again no more sleep and all the while the Gray Man is standing in the corner standing at the bed staring, his eyes a pair of long-dead stars staring, staring and all the while he is trying to speak.

"So, you and Allie still on the blink?"

"Yeah. Haven't heard from her since. Since. That night."

Saul laughed.

"The night you kicked her out of bed at three in the goddamn morning and told her to go home? I'm surprised she's not writing you sonnets." He shoved another onion ring in his mouth. It looked to Franco like a giant mouth stretched wide. Trying to speak.

"Yeah, yeah, I can't say I blame her. Not exactly. But. God, you have no idea what this is like, Saul. It's been a couple weeks since I've slept more than maybe an hour a night. And even that hour, I'm not sure of."

"Maybe you dreamt that hour," Saul said, and laughed again. Another onion ring, gone. It's urgent message lost down Saul's throat.

"Funny. You're funny. I cannot get over the funny. I got some pills this morning from the doctor. Something to help me sleep. I hope." Franco drove another bite of potato salad into his mouth. The Big Belly Deli usually had great potato salad. Today's offering was bland. Textureless. Like baby cereal. He grabbed at the salt again, dosed the salad liberally.

"Jeez," said Saul, "you want me to just grab you a salt lick?"

"Don't blame me. Blame the Deli. Forgot to season this stuff."

"I think it's gotta be twenty percent salt by volume, by now. Maybe you're coming down with something. Your sense of taste kinda goes when you've got a bug."

"Maybe. Maybe just the insomnia. Taste buds are asleep. Right. Anyway. We going again this weekend?"

"Yeah, totally. I'm surprised you're so into it. This is the first you've been gung-ho about one of my hobbies."

"It's the first time you've picked one that didn't suck. There's something about…you know. When you're underground. Looking at things that nobody but a handful of people has touched or even seen in decades. There's something almost intimate about it."

"Yeah, I don't want to fuck the Underground, I just want to check it out. I was looking at some maps and reading up a little. There's supposed to be this place, used to be a brothel back in the days. I thought maybe we could try to find it this weekend."

"You don't want to go back to the apartments?"

"We, uh, kinda saw everything there was to see down there, didn't we?"

Franco forced down a mouthful of gunk. It was like trying to swallow a sock.

"I guess you're right. Unless you wanted to try and get through that cinder block wall?"

"Uhhh, not really. Looked pretty solid. And I don't know if I'm too keen on pounding away at one of the walls that could be holding the ceiling over our heads, you know?"

"I guess. Brothel sounds cool."

"Maybe we'll find some fossilized panties or something."

Franco laughed. "Yeah." He looked around the tiny confines of the deli. "Is it dark in here?"

At 10:30 in the evening, Franco swallowed one little, beige pill from the prescription bottle marked "Zolpidem Tartrate, 10mg." He lay in bed alone and did a crossword puzzle. Waited for sleep to take him. Fifteen minutes later, he turned off the light and lay on his back. Five minutes after that, he slept.

The alarm clock blinked 6:00 am and chirped in its tinny, electronic voice; Franco awoke. He didn't recall waking even once during the night. All he could remember was a dream, of him standing in the Underground, staring at the cinderblock wall, then hefting a sledgehammer over his shoulder and bringing it down against that tiny, black eye. Again and again, and he sang tunelessly as he labored.

The dream was all that remained of the previous seven hours, and by the time he emerged from the shower, naked and dripping, even that was gone.

Saturday morning came and went. Franco's and Saul's trip into the Underground came and went. They had jogged leftward where before they had gone rightward, and with the aid of a dented compass Saul had bought long ago, they found the brothel.

There were no fossilized underwear, though there was an ancient, leather-bound ledger filled with the dust of former pages, and a room with a bed that could have told some tales. Despite four consecutive days of cadaverous sleep, Franco was exhausted. Still making up for several weeks of sleeplessness, he figured. It would pass.

As Saul stood before what remained of a subterranean brothel bed and mimed his ideas on what must've transpired there, Franco laughed, but most of him was somewhere else. Most of him stood beyond that gray, stone wall, stood before the man with the gray hair and the gray eyes and the gray smile. When he spoke, even his voice was gray.

Part of Franco laughed with his friend Saul amidst the dust and the grit, but most of him belonged to the Gray Man.

"Hello?"

"Where were you last night?"

"What? Allie, hi, what?"

"Last night. You weren't at home when I came by."

"Hun, I was here the whole night. I watched some television, at ten I went to bed. I woke up at six. You were never here."

"I came over last night just before midnight, I let myself in. I was going to surprise you, because I thought I'd been hard on you. I know you haven't been sleeping and I wanted to apologize and I thought we could, we could, and then I got there and, and I went into your room and you were *gone*, the bed was all rumpled up but you were *gone*."

"Allie, I swear, I was there the entire night. I—"

"Don't lie to me!"

"—got some pills to help me sleep and they've been *working*, they've been—"

"*DON'T LIE TO ME.* I was *there*, I saw the *bed* and you were fucking *gone*, I—"

"Babe, I swear, I, I was there all night. I went to sleep there and I woke up there, and—"

"If you're not going to admit it, then, then, fuck, then just, just *FUCK YOU*, God, fucking *lying to me, ASSHOLE.*"

There was a click, and she was gone.


Dark clouds filled the sky and the city below was a watercolor in sepia tones. A tiny bit of Franco, maybe the bit that still remembered sleep, held reservations about sinking into the Underground alone for the first time. Safety in numbers, Saul has said. Never go exploring alone. Just in case. It was safe, of course, perfectly safe, but never go alone.

Franco didn't want to wait until the weekend. Didn't want to bring Saul into this. Not just yet. Maybe later, but for now this was his problem.

His problem.

Perhaps that was true. Perhaps it was just the problem that was his, but perhaps there were other things Franco didn't yet want to share.

He had found dust in his bed.

After talking to Allie, Franco had dialed her number, and again, and then had given up and went into his bedroom. He had pulled the covers down and ground into the floral print sheets Allie had bought him were little patches of thick, gray grit. On the pillow, too, when he paid it close attention.

He always showered after he came back from the Underground. *Always.*

And he was still so tired all the time.

Arms sore.

Back hurt.

He found his way back to the sunken apartment building effortlessly. He had brought his own supply of glow sticks. Marked his path well. But something told him that he could probably find his way just fine even in the pregnant blackness. And after all, it wasn't so black anymore. More of a gray.

He saw the sledgehammer before he had even hit the bottom of the short, deteriorating stair. Standing against one wall. Balanced on its heft like an exclamation mark.

The cinderblock wall was gone.

Light from his flash washed over the scene like an apology, pushing feebly through the newly-formed doorway and illuminating nothing. Franco walked to the threshold and stood still. The path to the supply room was filled with excavated rubble.

Where had he even *gotten* a sledgehammer?

The dark sucked at him like a missing tooth. He walked forward.

The path wound downward. Not quite a hallway, not quite a cave. Something all its own, lined in stone that no more belonged here than the sledgehammer, no more than Franco himself.

Except that wasn't exactly true, was it?

Forward and down and the light of his flash seemed pointless, if anything it made it harder to see. Franco clicked the light off.

Better.

Sleek, gray stone hugged him on either side, above him. Caressing his feet like a lover. Contours stood out, etchings coursed down the tunnel in narrow rivulets of stone, like someone had drawn a comb over the surface when the rock was still molten. He ran a finger along one wall and it was smooth, like volcanic glass. Slightly warm.

The passage emptied out into a cavern the size of his bedroom only taller, obscene in its sheer height, and shouldn't there be city up there? Instead of empty space shouldn't there be streets and cars and pedestrians and general hubbub? How far had he walked? How far down?

There stood the Gray Man.

He was tall. Slight. He wore gray slacks and a gray shirt that only seemed to be there if you didn't quite look at them. They existed at the periphery of vision, of thought, where the subconscious met the conscious. So did the Gray Man. Franco had the impression that if he walked forward, he would pass right through him.

*Hello,* said the Gray Man. His mouth moved and sound appeared, but there seemed only a casual connection between the two. *You are here.*

"I'm here," said Franco. "Why? Why am I here?"

*We need you to be here need your help here need you here.*

"Who are you?"

*I am the one who waits. We need me here, too, need you and need me.*

The door wasn't much of a door. Wasn't a door at all, really – just an outline, vaguely rectangular. A jut of stone midway down might have been a knob. A concavity beside it might have been a keyhole.

"Where's that lead?" asked Franco, but he knew. It was where he needed to go. It was where he was meant to go.

*This is the door and you need the key I have the key can give you the key.*

The Gray Man pointed to the ground and Franco looked downward at a splinter of stone six inches long. He bent and picked it up. It was a stone in the same way a car is a slab of metal. It held purpose. Tiny depressions and ridges covered its surface, begging to be paired with the tumblers it was meant to manipulate. It glowed faintly.

Franco walked forward and felt he was just about to pass through the Gray Man, pass into him and become one with them and wouldn't that be terrible wonderful but the Man stepped aside and Franco instead found himself at the door.

*Close your eyes.*

Franco closed his eyes and found the key guiding itself to the lock, and even through closed eyes he could see it click into place, see it turn, see the door swing inwards and while his feet did not move still he fell beyond the doorway.

Beyond the doorway lay a small cavern, and from it stretched a narrow walkway. Everything was cast in brilliant shades of gray, blues and golds and reds and violets that were no part of any spectrum Franco had ever seen. Everything was gray and everything was filled with color and it burned his eyes burned his mind and Franco pulled the door shut slammed it shut and flung the key to the ground and ran, ran, ran back the way he had come, out of that searing monochrome nightmare, ran screaming the whole way, and he did not stop until he hit the surface and even for some time thereafter he screamed, sitting in the abandoned factory, and only after the screaming stopped did Franco realize his eyes were still closed.

...lying in bed, flat slab of ceiling blue-gray-black, shadows figures in the corners standing watch standing guard, can't sleep, can't sleep, mustn't use the pills, never the pills, the clock strikes one the clock strikes two the clock strikes three and that's it for me but no pills, no pills or he'll get me have me use me, never again except the *colors* dear God the *colors* and is it really so bad after all...

Saul was halfway through a bag of jerky when Franco scrabbled over the tatter of chainlink. Saul didn't worry often; it wasn't his style. Things had a way of working out, and time spent moping around was time spent not living.

When he saw his friend stomping through the mud, flashlight before him like a crucifix, he worried.

"Hey, Franco." His voice was gentle, almost lyrical, the sort of voice used against ledge-jumpers and froth-mouthed dogs.

"Saul." Franco's hair was flat against his skull and his long-sleeved shirt was torn and matted with grime. Eyes like nickels gleaming from the pit of an abandoned well. Short slash of mouth. "Thanks for showing up."

"Yeah, no problem. Listen, I'm, uh…what are we doing here exactly? Haven't heard from you in two weeks. You don't return my calls, the bank says you haven't been there since last Tuesday, and now…here you are."

"Here I am." Franco reached Saul and stopped. "Like I said, it's important. I have something to show you. I thought this was something just for me, but maybe it's not. Maybe it's meant to share." Franco's voice came at Saul as if through thick gauze.

"So, why *aren't* you at work?"

Franco coughed out a brittle laugh. "Maybe this is my work. Can anyone really say?" He waggled his light. "Let's go."

He walked through the garage door, but Saul stood fast.

"Are you sleeping? Those pills, they helping?"

"No pills," said Franco without stopping. "Better this way. C'mon."

Saul followed his lead. He pulled his light from his pack and flicked it on.

They were silent as they crept through the city's catacombs. Franco walked at a fevered pitch, and Saul asked him at times to slow down, but he never did. After several minutes, he noticed that Franco hadn't turned on his light.

"We aren't going through that cinderblock wall," said Saul. "I told

you, we whack at that thing and the whole city could fall down on us."
Franco didn't turn his head, but Saul could feel him smiling.

They were in the old apartment building now.

Across the foyer.

On the staircase, and then at its base, when Saul hissed:

"Christ, what did you *do?*"

"It wasn't me," said Franco. "It was the Gray Man. I was just the hammer."

Franco didn't break stride as he ducked into the passage and headed down the stone chute, but Saul did.

"I'm not going down there. No fucking way. Tell me what this is about first, or I'm...I'll..." Except he never finished the thought, because Franco was still heading downward and Saul was pulled after him like a dog leashed to a moving car.

In the tunnel.

At the end, now.

Franco stood against one wall like a game show hostess ready to gesture at fabulous prizes.

"This is it," said Franco in a voice Saul could barely hear. "See? This is what I needed to find."

"It's a cave, man. There's not even anything in here except rocks and some really stank air."

"You need to turn off your light, I think."

Saul did.

"Now it's a dark cave."

"No, see the door. Over here, the door."

"I can't see any door, Franco. I can't see anything, because *it is dark.* I'm turning my light back on."

The light blasted across the walls of the cave and Franco shrank back against the wall.

"Doesn't matter. I'll find the key. Let me find the...yes, here it is." Franco bent down and picked a jag of rock from the ground. "See? I have the key."

"You have a rock."

Franco pushed the rock against his door, tried to jab it into a tiny depression. The rock made small, dead noises as he stabbed it into the stone wall, *click-click-click*, like a death clock.

"It's not working. Why isn't it working? It's supposed to…" *Click.* "…open when I…" *Click.* "Do this." *Click. Clickclickclickclick.*

He shrugged. "No matter. There's probably a reason why it's not opening."

"Yeah, man, it's because *it is a fucking stone wall*, and you are *poking it with a fucking rock.*" Saul sighed and moved forward, put a hand on Franco's shoulder. It felt slight, like he was made of papier mache. "Look, you showed me your special cave, let's go back topside and talk about it. I'll listen to whatever you have to say, that's cool, but I don't like it down here."

"I can't tell you, Saul. You would think I was crazy if I tried."

*What the hell do you suppose I'm thinking about you now?* Saul didn't say. Instead:

"Just…just let's go. Okay?"

"It's beautiful in there, you know." His voice crawled across the stone. Saul was suddenly glad that he couldn't see Franco's face, those eyes.

"Is it."

"He needs me, you know. There's something in there, something important. I didn't get it at first. At first I was scared of him. The Gray Man. Can you believe it?"

"Yeah, I actually can. Look, can we—"

"Like skydiving, a little. You jump and you're terrified, everything's rushing at you and you're just so terrified, but afterward you stop and think and it doesn't seem so scary. And you just want to do it again."

"Franco, you hated skydiving. During, after, you hated it. Scared you fucking cross-eyed."

"You know what I realized, though? He's scared, too. Scared and tired and doesn't belong here not here. It'll all pass, though. The insomnia? It'll pass all pass all be over. Once I help him."

"Franco—"

"I wish I could make you see." Franco turned around and smiled. "But it's probably for the best that you can't."

"Let's just go, okay?"

Franco stared at the rock in his hand as if trying to will it into a key. Saul was just about to repeat himself when Franco turned, nodded, and started back the way they had come.

Another tunnel, this one done up in surgical greens and blues. Lots of doors, some of them open, most of them closed. Everything was a tunnel, now, to Saul. The hall leading to his apartment, Connor Street beneath the arc of trees clutching at their leaves in the autumn, the hospital wing he currently walked down. All tunnels, all looking to hold him for a time. Maybe not forever, but for a time.

He was done with urban exploration. Spelunking, too. All of it. He needed the sky. He wished he could see the sky now.

The call had come at four in the afternoon two days ago. Saul had answered his cell, and some slithering wisp of voice had said, "Everything is gone." Then silence.

He had almost driven to Franco's apartment, guided by sheer muscle memory, but he'd thought twice and driven to the factory instead. He'd seen Franco curled up in a patch of mud outside the garage door, wearing tattered remnants of the same grubby clothes he'd been wearing a week prior. His backpack was hiked up high on his shoulders, like it was trying to tear free.

He didn't move when Saul called his name, or shook him gently with his hand, or lifted his face and shouted into it as loud as he could. When he hiked Franco up over his shoulders, it was like lifting a Styrofoam replica.

The doctor pronounced him stable last night. Today he was eligible to receive visitors.

Saul ducked when he went through the door to Franco's room as if it was two feet shorter than it really was. He crept past the curtain, and wished distantly that he had a flashlight. He felt a crazy urge to mark his trail with glowsticks.

"Hey, Franco."

Franco sat in his bed, upright, hands folded in his lap. His eyes were open and clear. Hospital garb folded around his frame like a bag of coathangers.

"Franco?" Saul edged closer. "Franco? Hello?"

"Hello?" said Franco at last. "You need to move closer. Hearing's almost gone, you know." He spoke as if through a mouthful of porridge. Saul moved alongside the bed and took his friend's hand.

"Franco?" he said, louder.

"Saul! Glad you're here. Sorry you need to yell. Sorry my voice is screwy. I'm numb, you know. No feeling anywhere. Can't feel the words I'm making, can't really hear them, either."

"And your eyes?"

"Nope, that's gone, too. I can make out shapes sometimes. Mostly everything is gray. I expected that blindness would be more black, you know? But everything's gray. No sight, no hearing, no touch, no taste. I can still smell a little bit, though. They say my brain's fine, eyes and ears all fine. 'Hysterical sensory loss,' they call it. I think that's doctor-ese for 'Fuck if we know.'" His mouth opened and his body shook, and Saul realized he was trying to laugh.

"Franco, God, what happened? What did you do?"

"What I had to, Saul." Spit dribbled down his chin as he twitched his mouth into a grin. "It's done, though. I got it." He turned his head towards the room's single window, towards building tops and blue sky. On the sill beneath sat a small, rusted can. Once it might have held beans or corn. The top of the can was crushed into a crescent shape, like a moon. Or a smile.

"What is it?"

"It needed saving. I can protect it here. He can't get it here."

"Who? The Gray Man?"

164

"No," said Franco, and his smile fell away. Only the can smiled now. Saul turned his head so he couldn't see it.

"No, not the Gray Man," Franco went on. "The other one."

"The other one who?"

"It's a funny place. Forgotten. It's old, Saul. You have no idea how old it is. I don't think they do, either. It's like the Underground, in a way. Do you think it's possible to build a new world on the remains of the old? And maybe they connect here and there. Where places are... thin." He spat laughter, or maybe he was coughing.

"I have no idea what you mean, Franco. Can you—"

"It should've been okay, you know. The Gray Man said so, and I think I believe him. Should've been okay, but I screwed up."

"Franco, I don't-"

"You still there, Saul? I can't hear you."

Saul raised his voice.

"I said—"

"Eh, guess it's gone. My ears. Think they just signed off for good. I trust you're still there, though. I need to keep hold of that thing, understand? I'll know if they take it. It still glows for me. It's the one thing I can still see. But I have no idea if they'll listen. Keep it with me. When I die, bury it with me. You understand?"

"What the hell happened to you down there? What did you *do?*"

And maybe Franco heard something after all, because he answered:

"I opened my eyes."

Franco slept. He doubted he could do it on his own even now, but the drugs took care of things. He assumed there were still drugs. There had been back when he could still feel, at any rate.

He wasn't sure if his eyes were open or closed. He sent the command from his brain to shut them just the same. Either way, he could see the glow of the thing he had rescued. It was safe. And Saul would take care of things, he had no doubt.

Franco slept, and his dreams were brilliant with color.

**Lyn Lifshin** is a widely-published poet and author of numerous books, including *The Licorice Daughter: My Year with Ruffian* (Texas Review Press); *Another Woman Who Looks Like Me* (Black Sparrow at David Godine); and *Barbaro: Beyond Brokenness* (Texas Review Press). Forthcoming books include *Tsunami as History* (Poetryrepairs.com) and *For the Roses: Poems for Joni Mitchell.*

---

## THE STEERAGE

*Stieglitz Photogravure*

My father tells us about leaving,
how on the night they left he had
to bring goats next door in the moon.
Since he was not the youngest, he
couldn't wait pressed under a shawl
of coarse cotton close to his mother's
breast as she whispered "hurry". Her
ankles were swollen from ten babies.
Though she was only 30 her ankles were
swollen from ten babies, her lank hair

hung in strings under the babushka she
swore she would burn in New York
City. She dreamt others pointed and
snickered near the tenement, that a
neighbor borrowed the only bowl that
was her mother's and broke it. That
night they left, every move had to be
secret. In rooms there was no heat
in, no one put on muddy shoes or talked.
It was forbidden to leave, a law they

*(continued)*

broke like the skin of ice on pails of milk.
Years from then, a daughter would write
that he didn't have a word for *America*
yet, that night of a new moon. His
mother pressed his brother to her, warned
everyone even the babies must not make
a sound. Frozen branches creaked. My
father shivered at men with guns near
straw roofs on fire. It took their old samovar,

every coin to bribe someone to take them
to the train. "Pretend to be sleeping," his
father whispered as the conductor moved
near. His mother stuffed cotton in the baby's
mouth. She held the mortar and pestle wrapped
in his quilt of feathers closer, told him
he would sleep in this soft blue in the years
ahead. But that night in steerage, he was
knocked sideways into the ribs of the boat so
sea sick he couldn't swallow the orange some
one threw from an upstairs bunk tho it was
bright as sun and smelled of a new country
he could only imagine though never how his
mother would become a stranger to herself
there, forget why they risked dogs and guns
to come

BIG PULP is a modern amalgam of the classic newstand of the Golden Age of pulp and popular fiction, where lucky readers could find literally dozens of magazines catering to all manner of interests and tastes.

BIG PULP mixes genres to offer the best SF mystery, horror, & fantasy from established and emerging genre writers from around the globe. Every edition is packed with great fiction of all kinds. Don't miss an issue!

ISBN# 0983644934

### Summer 2012: The Purloined Pearl

An Indonesian fisherman steals a dragon's pearl for his lover, but their avarice takes a grievous toll on all they hold dear, in James Penha's "The Purloined Pearl," the featured story in the Summer 2012 issue of Big Pulp (cover art by Pete Schmitt). This issue also features more than 25 SF, fantasy, mystery and horror stories and poems.

For contents and ordering details, visit: www.exterpress.com/bigpulp/summer2012

ISBN# 0983644926

### Spring 2012: The Biggin Hill Duel

A British detective with a keen sense of ratiocination tackles one of his strangest cases in Adrian Ludens' steampunk mystery "The Biggin Hill Duel," the cover feature to the Spring 2012 issue of Big Pulp (cover by Ken Knudtsen). In all, this issue features 25 SF, fantasy, mystery and horror stories and poems.

For contents and ordering details, visit: www.exterpress.com/bigpulp/spring2012

**BIG PULP**

interrogate my heart instead
by elehah steinke

ISBN# 983644918

## Winter 2011: Interrogate My Heart Instead

An Iranian dissident confronts his torturer and former lover in Elaheh Steinke's "Interrogate My Heart Instead," the featured story in the Winter 2011 issue of Big Pulp (cover by Ken Knudtsen). This issue also features more than 25 SF, fantasy, mystery and horror stories and poems.

For contents and ordering details, visit: www.exterpress.com/bigpulp/winter2011

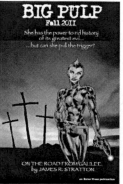

**BIG PULP**
Fall 2011

She has the power to rid history
of its greatest evil...
...but can she pull the trigger?

ON THE ROAD FROM GALILEE
by JAMES R. STRATTON

ISBN# 098364490X

## Fall 2011: On the Road from Galilee

A scientist travels back in time to rid history of one of its greatest evils, but when the time comes, will she be able pull the trigger? Find out in "On the Road from Galilee," the cover feature of the Fall 2011 issue of Big Pulp (cover art by Robert Hand). This issue features more than 20 SF, fantasy, mystery and horror stories and poems.

For contents and ordering details, visit: www.exterpress.com/bigpulp/fall2011

**BIG PULP**
Winter 2010

ted bundy's beetle
by Jarrid Deaton

sku# bp201012

## Winter 2010: Ted Bundy's Beetle

First issue! When a used car dealer acquires the infamous Volkswagen owned by serial killer Ted Bundy, his business booms, but with unintended consequences, in Jarrid Deaton's taut psychological thriller, "Ted Bundy's Beetle," the featured story in the Winter 2010 issue of Big Pulp. This issue features more than 25 SF, fantasy, mystery and horror stories and poems.

For contents and ordering details, visit:

CPSIA information can be obtained at www.ICGtesting.com
Printed in the USA
BVOW071918030912

299349BV00001B/10/P